ANYWHEN

Each of the stories in this book was directly commissioned by a magazine editor, an opportunity I used
in each case to try an experiment of one kind or another.
I've used this collection to second-guess one of the
experiments, as follows:

In September of 1965, Kyril Bonfiglioli found himself
host in Oxford to five science-fiction writers (Brian W.
Aldiss, Poul Anderson, James G. Ballard, Harry
Harrison, and myself) and an artist (Judith Ann
Lawrence), and commissioned from us all material for
what was to be the first issue of *Impulse*, a successor
(now defunct) to England's long-established professional magazine *Science-Fantasy*. The five stories and
the cover were all to develop the theme of a man who
sacrifices his life for a cause—or who doesn't. Except
for this bare statement, which as I recall was Mr.
Aldiss' suggestion, we had no other instructions except
(for the writers) to stay inside ten thousand words.

My contribution to that "OxCon issue" was a
novelette called "A Hero's Life". It was written in a
vast hurry to meet Mr. Bonfiglioli's deadline, and I
didn't realize until too late to start something else that
I had too much material to fit comfortably inside ten
thousand words. Hence, I've taken the opportunity to
rewrite it, as the novella which leads off this book.

Treetops, Woodlands Road,   JAMES BLISH
Harpsden (Henley), Oxon
1970

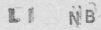

James Blish

ANYWHEN

ARROW BOOKS

Arrow Books Limited
3 Fitzroy Square, London W1

An imprint of the Hutchinson Publishing Group

London Melbourne Sydney Auckland
Wellington Johannesburg and agencies
throughout the world

First published in Great Britain by Faber & Faber Ltd 1971
Arrow edition 1978
© James Blish 1956, 1960, 1961, 1962, 1965,
1966, 1967, 1968, 1971

Made and printed in Great Britain
by The Anchor Press Ltd
Tiptree, Essex

ISBN 0 09 916000 5

To
HARRY HARRISON
a good companion

Contents

A Style in Treason

CHAPTER ONE

The *Karas*, a fragile transship—she was really little more than a ferry, just barely meriting a name—came fluttering out of the interstitium into the Flos Campi system a day late in a ball of rainbows, trailing behind her two gaudy contrails of false photons, like a moth unable to free herself of her cocoon. The ship's calendar said it was Joni 23, 5914, which was probably wrong by at least ten years; however, nobody but a scholar of that style of dating could have been precise about the matter; the *Karas* was a day later than she should have been; just *what* day was at best only a local convention.

In the salon, Simon de Kuyl sighed and laid out the tarots again. Boadacea, the biggish fourth planet of the Flos Campi array and Simon's present port of call, was yet a week ahead in urspace, and he was already tired. He had reasons. His fellow passengers had been dull beyond belief, with the possible—because wholly unknown—exception of the entity who had spent the entire voyage in his cabin, with a diplomatic seal spidered over the palm plate on its door; and Simon suspected that they would have bored him even had he not had to present himself to them as a disillusioned Sagittarian mystic, embittered at himself for ever having believed that the Mystery that lay (or didn't lie) at the galactic centre would someday emerge and set the rest of the universe to rights, and hence in too unpredictable a temper to be worth being polite to. Conceivably, indeed probably, some of the other passengers were trying to be as repellent

13

to strangers as was Simon, but the probability did not make their surfaces any more diverting.

But of course none of these things—the ship, the delay, the passengers, the pose—was more than marginally to blame for his weariness. In these days of treason, politeness, easy travel, and indefinitely prolonged physical vigour, everyone was tired, just a little but all the time. After a while, it became difficult to remember who one was supposed to be—and to remember who one was, was virtually impossible. Even the Baptized, who had had their minds dipped and then rechannelled with only a century's worth of memories, betrayed to the experienced eye a vague, tortured puzzlement, as though still searching in the stilled waters for some salmon of ego they had been left no reason to suspect had ever been there. Suicide was unconcealedly common among the Baptized, and Simon did not think the reason (as the theoreticians and ministers insisted) was really only a minor imperfection in the process, to be worked out in time.

There was plenty of time; that was the trouble. People lived too damn long, that was all. Erasing the marks, on the face or in the mind, did not unwind the years; the arrow of entropy pointed forever in the same direction; virginity was a fact, not just a state of membrane or memory. Helen, reawakening in Aithra's Egyptian bed flensed of her history, might bemuse Menelaus for a while, but there will always be another Paris, and that without delay—time past is eternally in time present, as Ezra-Tse had said.

The ten-thousand-year-old analogy came easily to him. He was supposed to be, and in fact was, a native of High Earth; and in his *persona* as a Sagittarian (lapsed) would be expected to be a student of such myths, the more time-dimmed the better—hence, in fact, his interminable shipboard not-quite-game of tarot solitaire. Staying quite automatically in character was in his nature, as well as being one of his chiefest skills.

And certainly he had never allowed himself to be Bap-

14

tized, though his mind had been put through not a few lesser changes in the service of High Earth, and might yet be forced into a greater one if his mission on Boadacea went awry. Many of his memories were painful, and all of them were painfully crowded together; but they were his, and that above all was what gave them their worth. Some professional traitors were valuable because they had never had, and never could have, a crisis of identity. Simon knew without vanity—it was too late for that—that High Earth had no more distinguished a traitor than he, precisely because he had such crises as often as once a year, and hadn't lost one yet.

"Your indulgence, reverend sir," said a voice at his back. A white hand, well kept but almost aggressively masculine, came over his shoulder and moved the Fool on to the Falling Tower. "It is boorish of me to intervene, but it discomforts me to see an implication go a-begging. I fear I am somewhat compulsive."

The voice was a new one: therefore, belonging to the person who had been sequestered in the diplomatic cabin up to now. Simon turned, ready to be surly.

His next impulse was to arise and run. The question of *who* the creature was evaporated in recognition of just *what* it was.

Superficially, he saw a man with a yellow page-boy coiffure, wearing pale-violet hose, short russet breeches, and a tabard of deeper violet, as well as a kangaroo-shiv, a weapon usually affected only by ladies. A duplicate of the spider on the doorseal was emblazoned in gold on his left breast. Superficially; for Simon was fortunate—in no way he could explain—to be able to penetrate this seeming.

The "diplomat" was a vombis, or what in those same myths Simon had been thinking of earlier was called a Proteus: a creature which could imitate perfectly almost any life-form within its size range. Or nearly perfectly; for Simon, like one in perhaps five thousand of his colleagues, was sensitive to them, without ever being able to specify in

15

what particular their imitations of humanity were deficient. Other people, even those of the sex opposite to the one the vombis had assumed, could find no flaw in them. In part because they did not revert when killed, no human had ever seen their "real" form—if they had one—though of course there were legends aplenty. The talent might have made them ideal double agents, had it been possible to trust them—but that was only an academic speculation, since the vombis were wholly creatures of the Green Exarch.

Simon's third impulse, like that of any other human being in like circumstances, was to kill this one instantly upon recognition, but that course had too many obvious draw-backs, of which the kangaroo-shiv was the least important. Instead, he said with only moderate ungraciousness: "No matter. I was blocked anyhow."

"You are most kind. May I be seated?"

"Since you're here."

"Thank you." The creature sat down gracefully, across the table from Simon. "Is this your first trip to Boadacea, reverend sir?"

Simon had not said he was going to Boadacea, but after all, it was written on the passenger list for anyone to see.

"Yes. And you?"

"Oh, that is not my destination; I am for deeper into the cluster. But you will find it an interesting world—especially the variations in the light; they make it seem quite dreamlike to a native of a planet with only a single, stable sun. And then, too, it is very old."

"What planet isn't?"

"I forget, you are from High Earth, to whom all other worlds must seem young indeed. Nevertheless, Boadacea is quite old enough to have many curious nations, all fiercely independent, and a cultural pattern which overrides all local variations. To this all the Boadaceans are intensely loyal."

"I commend them," Simon said; and then added sourly, "it is well for a man to have a belief he can cling to."

16

"The point is well taken," said the vombis. "Yet the pride of Boadacea springs from disloyalty, in the last analysis. The people believe it was the first colony to break with Old Earth, back in the first days of the Imaginary Drive. It is a breach they mean to see remains unhealed."

"Why not?" Simon said, shrugging. "I'm told also that Boadacea is very wealthy."

"Oh, excessively; it was once a great temptation to raiders, but the nations banded together against them with great success. Yet surely wealth does not interest you, reverend sir?"

"Marginally, yes. I am seeking some quiet country in which to settle and study. Naturally, I should prefer to find myself a patron."

"Naturally. I would suggest, then, that you try the domain of the Rood-Prince. It is small and stable, the climate is said to be clement, and he has a famous library." The creature arose. "For your purposes I would avoid Druidsfall; life there, as in most large cities, might prove rather turbulent for a scholar. I wish you success, reverend sir."

Placing its hand formally upon the jewelled shiv, the creature bowed slightly and left. Simon remained staring down at his cards, thinking icily but at speed.

What had all that meant? First of all, that his cover had been broken? Simon doubted that, but in any event it mattered little, since he would go almost into the open directly after landing. Assuming that it had, then, what had the creature been trying to convey? Surely not simply that life in Druidsfall would be even more turbulent for a traitor than for a lapsed divine. Naturally, it would expect Simon to know that; after all, Druidsfall was the centre of the treason industry on Boadacea—that was why Simon was going there.

Or was it that Boadacea would be difficult for an ordinary traitor to buy, or was not for sale at all? But that might be said of any worthwhile planet, and no professional would

17

let such a reputation pass without testing it, certainly not on the unsupported word of a stranger.

Besides, Simon was after all no ordinary traitor, nor even the usual kind of double agent. His task was to buy Boadacea while seeming to sell High Earth, but beyond that, there was a grander treason in the making for which the combined Traitors' Guilds of both planets might only barely be sufficient: the toppling of the Green Exarch, under whose subtle, nonhuman yoke half of humanity's worlds had not even the latter-day good sense to groan. For such a project, the wealth of Boadacea was a prerequisite, for the Green Exarch drew tithes from six fallen empires older than man— the wealth of Boadacea, and its reputation, which the vombis had invoked, as the first colony to have broken with Old Earth.

And such a project would necessarily be of prime interest to a creature of the Exarch. Yet security on it could not possibly have been broken. Simon knew well that men had died horribly for travelling under such assumptions in the past; nevertheless, he was sure of it. Then what—?

A steward walked slowly through the salon, beating a gong, and Simon put the problem aside for the moment and gathered up his cards.

"Druidsfall. One hour to Druidsfall. All passengers for the Flos Campi system please prepare for departure. Druidsfall in one hour; next port of call is Fleurety."

The Fool, he thought, has come to the Broken Tower. The next card to turn might well be the Hanged Man.

CHAPTER TWO

Boadacea proved indeed to be an interesting world, and despite all of Simon's preliminary reading and conditioning, quite as unsettling as the vombis had predicted.

Its sun, Flos Campi, was a ninety-minute microvariable, twinned at a distance of one light-year with a blue-white,

Rigellike star which stood—or had stood throughout historical times—in high southern latitudes. This meant that every spot on the planet had a different cycle of day and night. Druidsfall, for example, had only four consecutive hours of quasi-darkness at a time, and even during this period the sky was indigo rather than black at its deepest—and more often than not flaring with auroras, thanks to the almost incessant solar storms.

Everything in the city, as everywhere on Boadacea, bespoke the crucial importance of fugitive light, and the fade-out-fade-in weather that went with it, all very strange after the desert glare of High Earth. The day after the *Karas* had fluttered down had dawned in mist, which cold gales had torn away into slowly pulsating sunlight; then had come clouds and needlelike rain which had turned to snow and then to sleet—more weather in a day than the minarets of Jiddah, Simon's registered home town, saw in a six-month. The fluctuating light and wetness was reflected most startlingly by its gardens, which sprang up when one's back was turned and did not need so much to be weeded as actually fought. They were constantly in motion to the ninety-minute solar cycle, battering their elaborate flowerheads against back walls which were everywhere crumbling after centuries of such soft, implacable impacts. Half the buildings in Druidsfall glistened with their leaves, which were scaled with so much soft gold that they stuck to anything they were blown against—the wealth of Boadacea was based anciently in the vast amounts of uranium and other power-metals in its soil, from which the plants extracted the inevitable associated gold as radiation shielding for their spuriously tender genes. Everyone one saw in the streets of Druidsfall, or any other such city, was a mutation of some sort—if he was not an outworlder—but after a few days in the winds they were all half yellow, for the gold scales smeared off the flying leaves like butter. Everyone was painted with meaningless riches—the very bedsheets glittered ineradicably with

19

flakes of it; and brunettes—especially among the elaborate hair styles of the men—were at a premium.

Druidsfall proper was the usual low jumble of decayed masonry, slightly less ancient slums, and blank-faced offices, but the fact that it was also the home city of the Guild— hence wholly convenient, if not congenial, for Simon—gave it character. The traitors had an architectural style of their own, characterized by structures put together mostly of fragmented statues and petrified bodies fitted to each other like puzzle pieces or maps. Traitors on Boadacea had belonged to an honoured social class for seven hundred years, and their edifices made it known.

So did their style of dealing. Simon attended upon the planet's Traitor-in-Chief with all due promptness, wearing the clasp which showed him to be a brother, though an outworlder, and made himself and his errand known with almost complete truthfulness—certainly much more than custom would have demanded. His opposite number, Valkol "the Polite", a portly, jowly man in a black abah decorated only with the clasp, with a kindly and humorous expression into which were set eyes like two bites of an iceberg, turned him out of the Guildhall with only as much courtesy as fraternal protocol strictly required—that is, twelve days to get off the planet.

Thus far, at least, the vombis had proven to be right about the Boadaceans, to the letter. The spirit remained to be tested.

Simon found an inn in which to lick his wounds and prepare for departure, as was permitted. Of course he had no intention of leaving; he was simply preparing to go to ground. Nevertheless, he had wounds to lick: After only four clockless days on Boadacea, he had already been driven into changing his residence, his methods, and his identity. It was a humiliating beginning.

CHAPTER THREE

Methods next. Listening automatically for the first sound of possible interruption, Simon emptied his little poisons into the catch basin in his new room, and ironically watched the wisps of wine-coloured smoke rise from the corroded maw of the drain. He was sorry to see them go; they were old, though venomous, friends; but a man's methods can be as telltale as a thumbprint, and now it would have to be assumed that Valkol had sent for, and would soon receive, some sort of dossier on Simon. The dossier would be wrong, but there was no predicting *wherein* it would be wrong; hence, out with the poisons, and all their cousins among Simon's apparatus. When assuming a new identity, the very first rule is: *Strip!*

The almost worn-away maker's legend on the catch basin read: *Julius, Boadacea*. Things made on this planet were usually labelled that generally, as though any place in the world were like any other, but this was both true and not true. Druidsfall was unmistakably Boadacean, but as the central city of the traitors it was also distinctively itself. Those buildings with their curtain walls of petrified corpses, for instance. . . .

Luckily, custom now allowed Simon to stay clear of those grim monuments, now that the first, disastrous formalities were over, and seek his own bed and breakfast. In the old, disinterestedly friendly inns of Druidsfall, the anonymous thumps and foreign outcries of the transients—in death, love, or trade—are said to make the regular lodgers start in their beds with their resident guilts. Of course all inns are like that, but nevertheless, that was why traitors liked to quarter there rather than in the Traitors' Halls run by the fraternity: It guaranteed them privacy, and at the same time helped them to feel alive. There is undoubtedly something inhibiting about trying to deal within walls pieced together of broken stone limbs, heads, and torsos, some of which had clearly been alive when the foundations were being dug and the scaffolding bolted together.

Thus, here in The Skopolamander, Simon could comfortably await his next contact, now that he had dumped his poisons. This—if there was to be one—would of course have to come about before the end of his immunity period. "Quarantine" was perhaps a more appropriate term.

No, the immunity was real, however limited, for as a traitor to High Earth he had special status. High Earth, the Boadaceans thought, was not necessarily Old Earth—but not necessarily *not*, either. For the rest of his twelve days, Simon would not be killed out of sheer conservatism, at least, though nobody official would attempt to deal with him, either.

He had eight of those days still to run—a dull prospect, since he had already completed every possible preliminary to going to ground, and spiced only by the fact that he had yet to figure out how long a day might officially be. The rhythms of Flos Campi offered no reliable clues his Sol-tuned diurnalism could read. At the moment there was nothing lighting the window of the room but an aurora, looking like a curtain of orange and hazy blue fire licking upward along a bone trestle. Radio around here, and probably even electrical power, must be knocked out as much as half the time, with so much stray magnetism washing back and forth. That might prove useful; he filed the thought.

In the meantime, there went the last of the poisons. Simon poured water from an amphora into the catch basin, which promptly hissed like a dragon just out of the egg and blurted a mushroom of cold blue steam which made him cough. *Careful!* he thought; acid after water, never water after acid—I am forgetting the most elementary lessons. I should have used wine. Time for a drink, in Gro's name!

He caught up his cloak and went out, not bothering to lock the door. He had nothing worth stealing but his honour, which was in his right hip pocket. Oh, and of course, High

Earth—that was in his left. Besides, Boadacea was rich: one could hardly turn around without knocking over some heap of treasures, artifacts of a millennium which nobody had sorted for a century, or even wanted to be bothered to sort. Nobody would think to steal from a poor traitor any object smaller than a king, or, preferably, a planet.

In the tavern below, Simon was joined at once by a playwoman.

"Are you buying tonight, excellence?"

"Why not?" And in fact he was glad to see her. She was blonde and ample, a relief from the sketchy women of the Respectables, whom fashion made look as though they suffered from some nervous disease that robbed them of appetite. Besides, she would exempt him from the normal sort of Boadacean polite conversation, which consisted chiefly of elaborately involuted jokes at which it was considered gauche to laugh. The whole style of Boadacean conversation, for that matter, was intended to be ignored; gambits were a high art, but end games were a lost one. Simon sighed and signalled for beakers.

"You wear the traitors' clasp," she said, sitting across from him, "but not much tree gold. Have you come to sell us High Earth?"

Simon did not even blink; he knew the query to be a standard opening with any outworlder of his profession.

"Perhaps. But I'm not on business at the moment."

"Of course not," the girl said gravely, her fingers playing continuously with a sort of rosary tasselled with two silver phalluses. "Yet I hope you prosper. My half-brother is a traitor, but he can find only small secrets to sell—how to make bombs, and the like. It's a thin life; I prefer mine."

"Perhaps he should swear by another country."

"Oh, his country is well worth selling, but his custom is poor. Neither buyer nor seller trusts him very far—a matter of style, I suppose. He'll probably wind up betraying some colony for a thousand beans and a fishball."

"You dislike the man—or is it the trade?" Simon said. "It seems not unlike your own, after all: One sells something one never really owned, and yet one still has it when the transaction is over, as long as both parties keep silent."

"You dislike women," the girl said, tranquilly, as a simple observation, not a challenge. "But all things are loans—not just chastity and trust. Why be miserly? To 'possess' wealth is as illusory as to 'possess' honour or a woman, and much less gratifying. Spending is better than saving."

"But there are rank orders in all things, too," Simon said, lighting a kief stick. He was intrigued in spite of himself. Hedonism was the commonest of philosophies in the civilized galaxy, but it was piquant to hear a playwoman trotting out the mouldy clichés with such fierce solemnity. "Otherwise we should never know the good from the bad, or care."

"Do you like boys?"

"No, that's not one of my tastes. Ah, you will say that I don't condemn boy-lovers, and that values are in the end only preferences? I think not. In morals, empathy enters in, eventually."

"So, you wouldn't corrupt children, and torture revolts you. But you were made that way. Some men are not so handicapped. I meet them now and then." The hand holding the looped beads made a small, unconscious gesture of revulsion.

"I think *they* are the handicapped, not *I*—most planets hang their moral imbeciles, sooner or later. But what about treason? You didn't answer that question."

"My throat was dry . . . thank you. Treason, well—it's an art; hence, again, a domain of taste or preference. Style is everything; that's why my half-brother is so inept. If tastes changed he might prosper, as I might had I been born with blue hair."

"You could dye it."

"What, like the Respectables?" She laughed, briefly but unaffectedly. "I am what I am; disguises don't become me.

Skills, yes—those are another matter. I'll show you, when you like. But no masks."

Skills can betray you too, Simon thought, remembering that moment at the Traitors' Guild when his proud sash of poison shells, offered in service, had lost him in an instant every inch of altitude over the local professionals that he had hoped to trade on. But he only said again, "Why not?" It would be as good a way as any to while away the time; and once his immunity had expired, he could never again trust a playwoman on Boadacea.

She proved, indeed, very skilful, and the time passed . . . but the irregular pseudo-days—the clock in the tavern was on a different time than the one in his room, and neither even faintly agreed with his High Earth-based chronometer and metabolism—betrayed him. He awoke one morning/noon/night to find the girl turning slowly black beside him, in the last embrace of a fungal toxin he would have reserved for the Emperor of Canes Venatici, or the worst criminal in human history.

His immunity period was up, and war had been declared. He had been notified that if he still wanted to sell High Earth, he would first have to show his skill at staying alive against the whole cold malice of all the Traitors of Boadacea.

CHAPTER FOUR

"How the Exarchy or the prehuman interstellar empires were held together is unknown, but in human history, at least, the bureaucratic problems of managing large stellar holdings from a single centre of government have proven to be insoluble. Neither the ultraphone nor the Imaginary Drive permitted the extension of human hegemony over a radius of more than ten light-years, a fact the colonies outside this sphere were not slow to appreciate and put to use. Luckily, a roughly uniform interstellar economy was maintained by tacit agreement after the political separations, since it was not widely recognized then—or now—that this much older invention can enforce a more thorough rule than can any personal or party autocracy.

"In this connection, one often hears laymen ask, Why do the various worlds and nations employ professional traitors when it is known that they are traitors? Why would they confide to the traitors any secret valuable enough to be sold to a third party? The answer is the same, and the weapon is the same: money. The traitors act as brokers in a continuous interstellar bourse on which each planet seeks to gain a *financial* advantage over the other. Thus the novice should not imagine that any secret put into his hands is exactly what it is said to be, particularly when its primary value purports to be military. He should also be wary of the ruler who seeks to subvert him into personal loyalty, which tears the economic tissue and hence should be left in the domain of untrained persons. For the professional, loyalty is a tool, not a value.

"The typical layman's question cited above should of course never be answered."

—"Lord Gro": *The Discourses*, Bk. I, Ch. LVII

Simon holed up quickly and drastically, beginning with a shot of transduction serum—an almost insanely dangerous expedient, for the stuff not only altered his appearance but his very heredity, leaving his head humming with false memories and false traces of character, derived from the unknowable donors of the serum, which conflicted not only with his purposes but even with his tastes and motives.

Under interrogation, he would break down into a babbling crowd of random voices, as bafflingly scrambled as his karyotypes, blood groups, and retina- and fingerprints. To the eye, his gross physical appearance would be a vague, characterless blur of many roles—some of them derived from the DNA of persons who had died a hundred years ago and at least that many parsecs away in space.

But unless he got the antiserum within fifteen High Earth days, he would forget first his mission, then his skills, and at last his very identity. Nevertheless, he judged that the risk had to be taken; for effete though some of the local traitors (always excepting Valkol the Polite) seemed to be, they were obviously quite capable of penetrating any lesser cover—and equally obviously, they meant business.

The next problem was how to complete the mission itself —it would not be enough just to stay alive. High Earth did not petrify failed traitors and mortar them into walls, but it had its own ways of showing displeasure. Moreover, Simon felt to High Earth a certain obligation—not loyalty, Gro forbid, but, well, call it professional pride—which would not let him be retired from the field by a backwater like Boadacea. Besides, finally, he had old reasons for hating the Exarchy; and hatred, unaccountably, Gro had forgotten to forbid.

No: It was not up to Simon to escape the Boadaceans. He had come here to gull them, whatever they might currently think of such a project.

And therein lay the difficulty; for Boadacea, beyond all other colony worlds, had fallen into a kind of autumn cannibalism. In defiance of that saying of Ezra-Tse, the edge was attempting to eat the centre. It was this worship of independence, or rather, of autonomy, which had not only made treason respectable, but had come nigh on to ennobling it . . . and was now imperceptibly emasculating it, like the statues one saw everywhere in Druidsfall which had been defaced and sexually mutilated by the grey disease of time and the weather.

Today, though all the Boadaceans proper were colonials in ancestry, they were snobs about their planet's prehuman history, as though they had not nearly exterminated the aborigines themselves but were their inheritors. The few shambling Charioteers who still lived stumbled through the streets of Druidsfall loaded with ritual honours, carefully shorn of real power but ostentatiously deferred to on the slightest occasion which might be noticed by anyone from High Earth. In the meantime, the Boadaceans sold each other out with delicate enthusiasm, but against High Earth —which was not necessarily Old Earth, but not necessarily *not*, either—all gates were formally locked.

Formally only, Simon and High Earth were sure, for the hunger of treason, like lechery, tends to grow with what it feeds on, and to lose discrimination in the process. Boadacea, like all forbidden fruits, should be ripe for the plucking, for the man with the proper key to its neglected garden.

The key that Simon had brought with him, that enormous bribe which should have unlocked Valkol the Polite like a child's bank, was temporarily useless. He would have to forge another, with whatever crude tools could be made to fall to hand. The only one accessible to Simon at the moment was the dead playwoman's gently despised half-brother.

His name, Simon had found out from her easily enough, was currently Da-Ud tam Altair, and he was Court Traitor to a small religious principate on the Gulf of the Rood, on the InContinent, half the world away from Druidsfall. Remembering what the vombis aboard the *Karas* had said about the library of the Rood-Prince, Simon again assumed the robes of a worn-out Sagittarian divine in search of a patron, confident that his face, voice, stance, and manner were otherwise utterly unlike his shipboard *persona*, and boarded the flyer to the InContinent prepared to enjoy the trip.

There was much to enjoy. Boadacea was a good-sized world, nearly ten thousand miles in diameter, and it was rich in more than money. Ages of weathering and vulcanism had broken it into many ecological enclaves, further diversified by the point-by-point uniqueness of climate contributed to each by the rhythmic inconstancies of Flos Campi and the fixity of Flos Campi's companion sun among the other fixed stars—and by the customs and colours of many waves of pioneers who had settled in those enclaves and sought to re-establish their private visions of the earthly paradise. It was an entirely beautiful world, could one but forget one's personal troubles long enough to really look at it; and the flyer flew low and slow, a procedure Simon approved despite the urgency the transduction serum was imposing upon the back of his mind.

Once landed by the Gulf, however, Simon again changed his plans and his outermost disguise; for inquiry revealed that one of the duties of the Court Traitor here was that of singing the Rood-Prince to sleep to the accompaniment of the sareh, a sort of gleeman's harp—actually a Charioteer instrument, ill-adapted to human fingers, which Da-Ud played worse than most of the Boadaceans who affected it. Simon therefore appeared at the vaguely bird-shaped palace of the Rood-Prince in the guise of a ballad merchant, and as such was enthusiastically received, and invited to catalogue the library; Da-Ud, the Rood-Prince said, would help him, at least with the music.

Simon was promptly able to sell Da-Ud twelve-and-a-tilly of ancient High Earth songs Simon had made up over-night—faking folk songs is not much of a talent—and had Da-Ud's confidence within an hour; it was as easy as giving Turkish Delight to a baby. He cinched the matter by throwing in free lessons on the traditional way to sing them.

After the last mangled chord had died, Simon asked Da-Ud quietly:

"By the way . . . (well sung, excellence) . . . did you know that the Guild has murdered your half-sister?"

Da-Ud dropped the imitation Charioteer harp with a noise like a spring-driven toy coming unwound.

"Jillith? But she was only a playwoman! Why, in Gro's name—"

Then Da-Ud caught himself and stared at Simon with sudden, belated suspicion. Simon looked back, waiting.

"Who told you that? Damn you—are you a Torturer? I'm not—I've done nothing to merit——"

"I'm not a Torturer, and nobody told me," Simon said. "She died in my bed, as a warning to me."

He removed his clasp from under the shoulder of his cloak and clicked it. The little machine flowered briefly into a dazzling actinic glare, and then closed again. While Da-Ud was still covering his streaming eyes, Simon said softly:

"I am the Traitor-in-Chief of High Earth."

It was not the flash of the badge that was dazzling Da-Ud now. He lowered his hands. His whole narrow body was trembling with hate and eagerness.

"What—what do you want of me, excellence? I have nothing to sell but the Rood-Prince . . . and a poor stick he is. Surely you would not sell me High Earth; I am a poor stick myself."

"I would sell you High Earth for twenty riyals."

"You mock me!"

"No, Da-Ud. I came here to deal with the Guild, but they killed Jillith—and that, as far as I'm concerned, disqualified them from being treated as civilized professionals, or as human beings at all. She was pleasant and intelligent, and I was fond of her—and besides, while I'm perfectly willing to kill under some conditions, I don't hold with throwing away an innocent life for some footling dramatic gesture."

"I wholly agree," Da-Ud said. His indignation seemed to be at least half real. "But what will you do? What *can* you do?"

"I have to fulfil my mission, any way short of my own death—if I die, nobody will be left to get it done. But I'd most dearly love to cheat, dismay, disgrace the Guild in the process, if it could possibly be managed. I'll need your help. If we live through it, I'll see to it that you'll turn a profit, too ; money isn't my first goal here, or even my second now."

"I'll tackle it," Da-Ud said at once, though he was obviously apprehensive, as was only sensible. "What, precisely, do you propose?"

"First of all, I'll supply you with papers indicating that I've sold you a part—not all—of the major thing I have to sell, which gives any man who holds it a lever in the State Ministry of High Earth. They show that High Earth has been conspiring against several major powers, all human, for purposes of gaining altitude with the Green Exarch. They won't tell you precisely which worlds, but there will be sufficient information there so that the Exarchy would pay a heavy purse for them—and High Earth, an even heavier one to get them back. It will be your understanding that the missing information is also for sale, but you haven't got the price."

"Suppose the Guild doesn't believe that?"

"They'll never believe—excuse me, I must be blunt—that you could have afforded the whole thing; they'll know I sold you *this* much of it only because I have a grudge, and you can tell them so—though I wouldn't expose the nature of the grudge, if I were you. Were you unknown to them, they might assume that you were me in disguise, but luckily they know you, and, ah, probably tend rather to under-estimate you."

"Kindly put," Da-Ud said with a grin. "But that won't prevent them from assuming that I know your whereabouts, or have some way of reaching you. They'll interrogate for that, and of course I'll tell them. I know them, too; it would be impossible not to, and I prefer to save myself needless pain."

"Of course—don't risk interrogation at all, tell them you want to sell me out, as well as the secret. That will make sense to them, and I think they must have rules against interrogating a member who offers to sell; most Traitors' Guilds do."

"True, but they'll observe them only so long as they believe me; that's standard, too."

Simon shrugged. "Be convincing, then," he said. "I have already said that this project will be dangerous; presumably,

31

you didn't become a traitor solely for sweet safety's sake."

"No, but not for suicide's, either. But I'll abide the course. Where are the documents?"

"Give me access to your Prince's toposcope-scriber and I'll produce them. But first—twenty riyals, please."

"Minus two riyals for the use of the Prince's property. Bribes, you know."

"Your sister was wrong. You do have style, in a myopic sort of way. All right, eighteen riyals—and then let's get on to real business. My time is not my own—not by a century."

"But how do I reach you thereafter?"

"That information", Simon said blandly, "will cost you those other two riyals, and cheap at the price."

CHAPTER FIVE

The Rood-Prince's brain-dictation laboratory was very far from being up to Guild standards, let alone High Earth's, but Simon was satisfied that the documents he generated there would pass muster. They were utterly authentic, and every experienced traitor had a feeling for that quality, regardless of such technical deficiencies as blurry image registration or irrelevant emotional overtones.

That done, he set himself in earnest to the task he had already been playing at, that of cataloguing the Rood-Prince's library. He could hardly run out on this without compromising Da-Ud, as well as drawing unwanted attention to himself. Happily, the chore was pleasant enough; in addition to the usual pornography, the Prince owned a number of books Simon had long wanted to see, including the complete text of Vilar's *The Apples of Idun*, and all two hundred cantos of Mordecai Drover's *The Drum Major and the Mask*, with the fabulous tipped-in Brock woodcuts, all hand-tinted. There were sculptures by Labuerre and Halvorsen; and among the music, there was the last sonata of Andrew Carr . . . all of this embedded, as was inevitable, in vast masses of junk; but of what library, large or small, might that *not* be said? Whether or not the Rood-Prince had taste, he certainly had money, and some of it, under some past librarian, had been well spent.

In the midst of all this, Simon had also to consider how he would meet Da-Ud when the game had that much furthered itself. The arrangement he had made with the playwoman's half-brother had of course been a blind, indeed a double blind; but it had to have the virtues of its imperfections—that is, to look as though it had been intended to work, and to work in fact up to a certain point—or nothing would be accomplished. And it would then have to be bailed out of its in-built fatalities. So—

But Simon was now beginning to find it hard to think. The transduction serum was increasingly taking hold, and there were treasons taking place inside his skull which had nothing at all to do with Da-Ud, the Rood-Prince, Druidsfall, Boadacea, the Green Exarch, or High Earth. Worse: They seemed to have nothing to do with Simon de Kuyl, either, but instead muttered away about silly little provincial intrigues nothing could have brought him to care about—yet which made him feel irritated, angry, even ill, like a man in the throes of jealousy towards some predecessor and unable to reason them away. Knowing their source, he fought them studiously, but he knew they would get steadily worse, however resolute he was; they were coming out of his genes and his blood-stream, not his once finely honed, now dimming consciousness.

Under the circumstances, he was not going to be able to trust himself to see through very many highly elaborate schemes, so that it would be best to eliminate all but the most necessary. Hence it seemed better, after all, to meet Da-Ud in the Principate as arranged, and save the double dealing for more urgent occasions.

On the other hand, it would be foolish to hang around the Principate, waiting and risking some miscarriage—such as betrayal through a possible interrogation of Da-Ud—when there were things he might be accomplishing elsewhere. Besides, the unvarying foggy warmth and the fragmented, garish religiousness of the Principate both annoyed him and exercised pulls of conflicting enthusiasms and loyalties on several of his mask personalities, who had apparently been as unstable even when whole as their bits and pieces had now made him. He was particularly out of sympathy with the motto graven on the lintel of the Rood-Prince's palace: JUSTICE IS LOVE. The sentiment, obviously descended from some colonial Islamic sect, was excellent doctrine for a culture knit together by treason, for it allowed the prosecution of almost any kind of betrayal on the grounds that justice (disguised as that kind of love which says, "I'm doing this for your own good; it hurts me more than it does you") was being pursued. But Simon, whose dimly remembered parents had betrayed him often on just those grounds, found it entirely too pat. Besides, he was suspicious of all abstractions which took the form "A is B". In his opinion, neither justice nor mercy were very closely related to love, let alone being identical with it—otherwise, why have three words instead of one? A metaphor is not a tautology.

These bagatelles aside, it seemed likely to Simon that something might be gained by returning for a while to Druidsfall and haunting the vicinity of the Guildhall. At the worst, his address would then be unknown to Da-Ud, and his anonymity more complete in the larger city, the Guild less likely to identify him even were it to suspect him—as of course it would—of such boldness. At best, he might pick up some bit of useful information, particularly if Da-Ud's embassy were to create any unusual stir.

Very well. Presenting the Rood-Prince with a vast stack of punched aperture cards and a promise to return, Simon took the flyer to Druidsfall, where he was careful to stay many miles away from The Skopolamander.

For a while he saw nothing unusual, which was in itself

fractionally reassuring. Either the Guild was not alarmed by Da-Ud's clumsy proposals, or was not letting it show. On several days in succession, Simon saw the Boadacean Traitor-in-Chief enter and leave, sometimes with an entourage, more often with only a single slave. Everything seemed normal, although it gave Simon a small, ambiguous *frisson* which was all the more disturbing because he was unsure which of his *personae* he should assign it to. Certainly not to his fundamental self, for although Valkol was here the predestined enemy, he was no more formidable than others Simon had defeated (while, it was true, being in his whole and right mind).

Then Simon recognized the "slave"; and this time he did run. It was the vombis, the same one who had been travelling as a diplomat aboard the *Karas*. The creature had not even bothered to change its face to fit its new role.

This time he could have killed the creature easily from his point of vantage, and probably gotten away clean, but again, there were compelling reasons for not doing so. Just ridding the universe of one of the protean entities (if it did any good at all, for nobody knew how they reproduced) would be insufficient advantage for the hue and cry that would result. Besides, the presence of an agent of the Exarchy so close to the heart of this imbroglio was suggestive, and might be put to some use.

Of course, the vombis might be in Druidsfall on some other business entirely, or simply paying a courtesy call on its way back from "deeper into the cluster"; but Simon would be in no hurry to make so dangerous an assumption. No, it was altogether more likely that the Exarch, who could hardly have heard yet of Simon's arrival and disgrace, was simply aware in general of how crucial Boadacea would be to any scheme of High Earth's—he was above all an efficient tyrant—and had placed his creature here to keep an eye on things.

Yes, that situation might be used, if Simon could just keep

his disquietingly percolating brains under control. Among his present advantages was the fact that his disguise was better than that of the vombis, a fact the creature had probably been made constitutionally incapable of suspecting by the whole thrust of its evolution.

With a grim chuckle which he hoped he would not later be forced to swallow, Simon flew back to the Gulf of the Rood.

CHAPTER SIX

Da-Ud met Simon in the Singing Gardens, a huge formal maze not much frequented of late even by lovers, because the Rood-Prince in the throes of some new religious crotchet had let it run wild, so that one had constantly to be fending off the ardour of the flowers. At best, this made even simple conversations difficult, and it was rumoured that deep in the heart of the maze the floral attentions to visitors were of a more sinister sort.

Da-Ud was exultant, indeed almost manic in his enthusiasm, which did not advance comprehension either, but Simon listened patiently.

"They bought it like lambs," Da-Ud said, naming a sacrificial animal of High Earth so casually as to make one of Simon's *personae* shudder inside him. "I had a little difficulty with the underlings, but not as much as I'd expected, and I got it all the way up to Valkol himself."

"No sign of any outside interest?"

"No, nothing. I didn't let out any more than I had to until I reached His Politeness, and after that he put the blue seal on everything—wouldn't discuss anything but the weather while anyone else was around. Listen, Simon, I don't want to seem to be telling you your business, but I think I may know the Guild better than you do, and it seems to me that you're underplaying your hand. This thing is worth *money*."

"I said it was."

"Yes, but I don't think you've any conception how much. Old Valkol took my asking price without a murmur—in fact, so fast that I wish I'd asked for twice as much. Just to show you I'm convinced of all this, I'm going to give it all to you."

"Don't want it," Simon said. "Money is of no use to me unless I can complete the mission. All I need now is operating expenses, and I've got enough for that."

This clearly had been what Da-Ud had hoped he would say, but Simon suspected that had matters gone otherwise, the younger man might indeed have given over as much as half the money. His enthusiasm mounted.

"All right, but that doesn't change the fact that we could be letting a fortune slip here."

"How much?"

"Oh, at least a couple of megariyals—and I mean *apiece,*" Da-Ud said grandly. "I can't imagine an opportunity like that comes around very often, even in the circles you're used to."

"What would we have to do to earn it?" Simon said, with carefully calculated doubt.

"Play straight with the Guild. They want the material badly, and if we don't trick them we'll be protected by their own rules. And with that much money, there are a hundred places in the galaxy where you'd be safe from High Earth for the rest of your life."

"And what about your half-sister?"

"Well, I'd be sorry to lose that chance, but cheating the Guild wouldn't bring her back, would it? And in a way, wouldn't it be *aesthetically* more satisfying to pay them back for Jillith by being scrupulously fair with them? 'Justice is Love', you know, and all that."

"I don't know," Simon said fretfully. "The difficulty lies in defining justice, I suppose—you know as well as I do that it can excuse the most complicated treasons. And 'What do you mean by love?' isn't easily answerable either. In the end, one has to shuck it off as a woman's question, too private to be meaningful in a man's world—let alone in matters of polity. Hmmmm."

This maundering served no purpose but to suggest that Simon was still trying to make up his mind; actually, he had reached a decision several minutes ago. Da-Ud had broken; he would have to be disposed of.

Da-Ud listened with an expression of polite bafflement which did not quite completely conceal a gleam of incipient triumph. Ducking a trumpet vine which appeared to be trying to crown him with thorns, Simon added at last: "You may well be right—but we'll have to be mortally careful. There may, after all, be another agent from High Earth here; in matters of this importance they wouldn't be likely to rest with only one charge in the chamber. That means you'll have to follow my instructions to the letter, or we'll never live to spend a riyal of the proceeds."

"You can count on me," Da-Ud said, tossing his hair out of his eyes. "I've handled everything well enough this time, haven't I? And, after all, it was my idea."

"Certainly. An expert production. Very well. What I want you to do now is go back to Valkol and tell him that I've betrayed you; and sold the other half of the secret to the Rood-Prince."

"Surely you wouldn't actually *do* such a thing!"

"Oh, but I *would*, and I *shall*—the deed will be done by the time you get back to Druidsfall, and for the same twenty riyals that you paid for your half."

"But the purpose——?"

"Simple. I cannot come to Druidsfall with my remaining half—if there's another Earthman there, I'd be shot before I got halfway up the steps of the Hall. I want the Guild to consolidate the two halves by what seems to be an unrelated act of aggression between local parties. You make this clear to them by telling them that I won't actually make the sale to the Rood-Prince until I hear from you that you have the rest of the money. To get the point across at once, when you tell His Politeness that I've 'betrayed' you—wink.''

"And how do I get word to you this time?"

"You wear this ring. It communicates with a receiver in my clasp. I'll take matters from there.''

The ring—which was actually *only* a ring, which would never communicate anything to anybody—changed hands. Then Da-Ud saluted Simon with solemn glee, and went away to whatever niche in history—and in the walls of the Guildhall of Boadacea—is reserved for traitors without style; and Simon, breaking the stalk of a lyre bush which had sprung up between his feet, went off to hold his muttering, nattering skull and do nothing at all.

CHAPTER SEVEN

Valkol the Polite—or the Exarch's agent, it hardly mattered which—did not waste any time. From a vantage point high up on the Principate's only suitable mountain, Simon watched their style of warfare with appreciation and some wonder.

Actually, in the manœuvring itself the hand of the Exarchy did not show, and did not need to; for the whole campaign would have seemed a token display, like a tournament, had it not been for a few score of casualties which seemed inflicted almost inadvertently. Even among these there were not many deaths, as far as Simon could tell—at least, not by the standards of battle to which he was accustomed.

Clearly, nobody who mattered got killed, on either side. It all reminded Simon of medieval warfare, in which the nearly naked kerns and gallowglasses were thrust into the front ranks to slaughter one another, while the heavily armoured knights kept their valuable persons well to the rear—except that here there was a good deal more trumpet blowing than there was slaughter. The Rood-Prince, in an exhibition of bravado more garish than sensible, deployed on the plain before his city several thousand pennon-bearing mounted troopers who had nobody to fight but a rabble of foot soldiers which Druidsfall obviously—at least, to Simon's eye—did not intend to be taken seriously; whereupon, the city was taken from the Gulf side, by a squadron of flying submarines which broke from the surface of the sea on four buzzing wings like so many dragonflies. The effect was like a raid by the twenty-fifth century upon the thirteenth, as imagined by someone in the twentieth—a truly dreamlike sensation.

The submarines particularly interested Simon. Some Boadaceous genius, unknown to the rest of the known galaxy, had solved the ornithopter problem—though the wings of the devices were membranous rather than feathered. Hovering, the machines thrummed their wings through a phase shift of a full hundred and eighty degrees, but when they swooped, the wings moved in a horizontal figure eight, lifting with a forward-and-down stroke, and propelling with the back stroke. A long, fish-like tail gave stability, and doubtless had other uses under water.

After the mock battle, the 'thopters landed and the troops withdrew; and then matters took a more sinister turn, manifested by thumping explosions and curls of smoke from inside the Rood palace. Evidently, a search was being made for the supposedly hidden documents Simon was thought to have sold, and it was not going well. The sounds of demolition, and the occasional public hangings, could only mean that a maximum interrogation of the Rood-Prince had failed to produce any papers, or any clues to them.

This Simon regretted, as he did the elimination of Da-Ud. He was not normally so ruthless—an outside expert would have called his workmanship in this affair perilously close to being sloppy—but the confusion caused by the transduction serum, now rapidly rising as it approached term, had prevented him from manipulating every factor as subtly as he had originally hoped to do. Only the grand design was still intact now: It would now be assumed that Boadacea had clumsily betrayed the Exarchy, leaving the Guild no way out but to capitulate utterly to Simon, with whatever additional humiliations he judged might not jeopardize the mission, for Jillith's sake—

Something abruptly cut off his view of the palace. He snatched his binoculars away from his eyes in alarm.

The object that had come between him and the Gulf was a mounted man—or rather, the idiot-headed apteryx the man was sitting on. Simon was surrounded by a ring of them, their lance points aimed at his chest, pennons trailing in the dusty viol grass. Someone of Simon's *personae* remembered that the function of a pennon is to prevent the lance from running all the way through the body, so that the weapon can be pulled out easily and used again, but Simon had more immediate terrors to engross him.

The pennons bore the device of the Rood-Prince; but every lancer in the force was a vombis.

Simon arose resignedly, with a token snarl intended more for himself than for the impassive protean creatures and their fat birds. He wondered why it had never occurred to him before that the vombis might be as sensitive to him as he was to them.

But the answer to that no longer mattered. Sloppiness was about to win its long-postponed reward.

CHAPTER EIGHT

They put him naked into a wet cell: a narrow closet completely clad in yellowed alabaster, down the sides of which water oozed and beaded all day long, running out into gutters at the edges. He was able to judge when it was day, because there were clouded bull's-eye lenses in each of the four walls which waxed and waned at him with any outside light. By the pattern of its fluctuation he could have figured out to a nicety just where on Boadacea he was, had he been in the least doubt that he was in Druidsfall. The wet cell was a sort of inverted oubliette, thrust high up into Boadacea's air, probably a hypertrophied merlon on one of the towers of the Traitors' Hall. At night, a fifth lens, backed by a sodium vapour lamp, glared down from the ceiling, surrounded by a faint haze of steam where the dew tried to condense on it.

Escape was a useless fantasy. Erected into the sky as it was, the wet cell did not even partake of the usual character of the building's walls, except for one stain in the alabaster which might have been the underside of a child's footprint; otherwise, the veinings were mockingly meaningless. The only exit was down, an orifice through which they had inserted him as though he were being born, and now plugged like the bottom of a stopped toilet. Could he have broken through one of the lenses with his bare hands, he would have found himself naked and torn on the highest point in Druidsfall, with no place to go.

Naked he was. Not only had they pulled all his teeth in search of more poisons, but of course they had also taken his clasp. He hoped they would fool with the clasp—it would make a clean death for everybody—but doubtless they had better sense. As for the teeth, they would regrow if he lived, that was one of the few positive advantages of the transduction serum, but in the meantime his bare jaws ached abominably.

They had missed the antidote, which was in a tiny gel capsule in his left earlobe, masquerading as a sebaceous cyst—left, because it is automatic to neglect that side of a man, as though it were only a mirror image of the examiner's right—and that was some comfort. In a few more days now, the gel would dissolve, he would lose his multiple disguise, and then he would have to confess, but in the meantime he could manage to be content despite the slimy, glaring cold of the cell.

And in the meantime, he practised making virtues of deficiencies: in this instance, calling upon his only inner resources—the diverting mutterings of his other personalities —and trying to guess what they might once have meant.

Some said:

"But I mean, like, you know——"

"Wheah they goin'?"

"Yeah."

"Led's gehdahda heah—he-he-he!"

"Wheah?"

"So anyway, so uh."

Others:

"It's hard not to recognize a pigeon."

"But Mother's birthday is 20th July."

"So he knew that the inevitable might happen——"

"It made my scalp creak and my blood curl."

"Where do you get those crazy ideas?"

And others:

"Acquit Socrates."

"Back when she was sane she was married to a window washer."

"I don't know what you've got under your skirt, but it's wearing white socks."

"And then she made a noise like a spindizzy going sour."

And others:

"Pepe Satan, pepe Satan aleppe."

"Why, so might any man."

"EVACUATE MARS!"

"And then she sez to me, she sez——"

". . . if he would abandon his mind to it."

"With all of love."

And . . . but at that point the plug began to unscrew, and from the spargers above him which formerly had kept the dampness running, a heavy gas began to curl. They had tired of waiting for him to weary of himself, and the second phase of his questioning was about to begin.

CHAPTER NINE

They questioned him, dressed in a hospital gown so worn
that it was more starch than fabric, in the Traitor-in-Chief's
private office to begin with—a deceptively bluff, hearty,
leather-and-piperacks sort of room, which might have been
reassuring to a novice. There were only two of them: Valkol
in his usual abah, and the "slave", now dressed as a
Charioteer of the high blood. It was a curious choice of
costume, since Charioteers were supposed to be free, leaving
it uncertain which was truly master and which slave; Simon
did not think it could have been Valkol's idea. The vombis,
he also noticed, still had not bothered to change its face
from the one it had been wearing aboard the *Karas*, implying
an utter confidence which Simon could only hope would
prove to be unjustified.

Noting the direction of his glance, Valkol said, "I asked
this gentleman to join me to assure you, should you be in
any doubt, that this interview is serious. I presume you
know who he is."

"I don't know who 'he' is," Simon said, with the faintest
of emphasis. "But it must be representing the Green Exarch,
since it's a vombis."

The Traitor-in-Chief's lips whitened slightly. Aha, then he
hadn't known that! "Prove it," he said.

"My dear Valkol," the creature interposed. "Pray don't
let him distract us over trifles. Such a thing could not be
proved without the most elaborate of laboratory tests, as we
all know. And the accusation shows what we wish to know,
i.e., that he is aware of who I am—otherwise, why try to
make such an inflammatory charge?"

"Your master's voice," Simon said. "Let us by all means
proceed—this gown is chilly."

"This gentleman", Valkol said, exactly as if he had
not heard any of the four preceding speeches, "is Chag
Sharanee of the Exarchy. Not from the Embassy, but directly
44

from the Court—he is His Majesty's Deputy Fomentor."

"Appropriate," Simon murmured.

"We know you now style yourself 'Simon de Kuyl', but what is more to the point, that you claim yourself the Traitor-in-Chief of High Earth. Documents now in my possession persuade me that if you are not in fact that officer, you are so close to being he as makes no difference. Possibly the man you replaced, the amateur with the absurd belt of poison shells, was actually he. In any event, you are the man we want."

"Flattering of you."

"Not at all," said Valkol the Polite. "We simply want the remainder of those documents, for which we paid. Where are they?"

"I sold them to the Rood-Prince."

"He had them not, nor could he be persuaded to remember any such transaction."

"Of course not," Simon said with a smile. "I sold them for twenty riyals; do you think the Rood-Prince would recall any such piddling exchange? I appeared as a bookseller, and sold them to his librarian. I suppose you burned the library—barbarians always do."

Valkol looked at the vombis. "The price agrees with the, uh, testimony of Da-Ud tam Altair. Do you think——?"

"It is possible. But we should take no chances; e.g., such a search would be time consuming."

The glitter in Valkol's eyes grew brighter and colder. "True. Perhaps the quickest course would be to give him over to the Sodality."

Simon snorted. The Sodality was a lay organization to which Guilds classically entrusted certain functions the Guild lacked time and manpower to undertake, chiefly crude physical torture.

"If I'm really who you think I am," he said, "such a course would win you nothing but an unattractive cadaver—not even suitable for masonry repair."

"True," Valkol said reluctantly. "I don't suppose you could be induced—politely—to deal fairly with us at this late date? After all, we did pay for the documents in question, and not any mere twenty riyals."

"I haven't the money yet."

"Naturally not, since the unfortunate Da-Ud was held here with it until we decided he no longer had any use for it. However, if upon the proper oaths——"

"High Earth is the oldest oath-breaker of them all," the Fomentor said. "We—viz., the Exarchy—have no more time for such trials. The question must be put."

"So it would seem. Though I hate to handle a colleague thus——"

"You fear High Earth," the vombis said. "My dear Valkol, may I remind you——"

"Yes, yes, the Exarch's guarantee—I know all that," Valkol snapped, to Simon's surprise. "Nevertheless—Mr. De Kuyl, are you *sure* we have no recourse but to send you to the Babble Room?"

"Why not?" Simon said. "I rather enjoy hearing myself think. In fact, that's what I was doing when your guards interrupted me."

CHAPTER TEN

Simon was, naturally, far from feeling all the bravado he had voiced, but he had no choice left but to trust to the transduction serum, which now had his mind on the shuddering, giddy verge of depriving all three of them of what they each most wanted. Only Simon, of course, could know this; and only he could also know something much worse— that in so far as his increasingly distorted time sense could calculate, the antidote was due to be released into his bloodstream at best in another six hours, at worst within only a few minutes. After that, the Exarchy's creature would be the only victor—and the only survivor.

And when he saw the Guild's toposcope laboratory, he wondered if even the serum would be enough to protect him. There was nothing in the least outmoded about it; Simon had never encountered its like even on High Earth. Exarchy equipment, all too probably.

Nor did the apparatus disappoint him. It drove directly down into his subconscious with the resistless unconcern of a spike penetrating a toy balloon. Immediately, a set of loud-speakers above his supine body burst into multi-voiced life:

"Is this some trick? No one but Berentz had a translation permit——"

"Now the overdrive my-other must woo and win me——"

"*Wie schaffen Sie es, solche Entfernungen bei Unterlicht-geschwindigkeit zurueckzulegen?*"

"REMEMBER THOR FIVE!"

"Pok. Pok. Pok."

"We're so tired of wading in blood, so tired of drinking blood, so tired of dreaming about blood——"

The last voice rose to a scream, and all the loudspeakers cut off abruptly. Valkol's face, baffled but not yet worried, hovered over Simon's, peering into his eyes.

"We're not going to get anything out of that," he told some invisible technician. "You must have gone too deep; those are the archetypes you're getting, obviously."

"Nonsense." The voice was the Fomentor's. "The arche-types sound nothing like that—for which you should be grateful. In any event, we have barely gone beneath the surface of the cortex; see for yourself."

Valkol's face withdrew. "Hmm. Well, *something's* wrong. Maybe your probe is too broad. Try it again."

The spike drove home, and the loudspeakers resumed their mixed chorus.

"*Nausentampen. Eddettompic. Berobsilom. Aimkaksetchoc. Sanbetogmow*——"

"*Dites-lui que nous lui ordonnons de revenir, en vertu de la Loi du Grand Tout.*"

"Perhaps he should swear by another country."

"Can't Mommy ladder spaceship think for bye-bye-see-you two windy Daddy bottle seconds straight——"

"*Nansima macamba yonso cakosilisa.*"

"Stars don't have points. They're round, like balls."

The sound clicked off again. Valkol said fretfully: "He can't be resisting. You've got to be doing something wrong, that's all."

Though the operative part of his statement was untrue, it was apparently also inarguable to the Fomentor. There was quite a long silence, broken only occasionally by small hums and clinks.

While he waited, Simon suddenly felt the beginnings of a slow sense of relief in his left earlobe, as though a tiny but unnatural pressure he had long learned to live with had decided to give way—precisely, in fact, like the opening of a cyst.

That was the end. Now he had but fifteen minutes more in which the toposcope would continue to vomit forth its confusion—its steadily diminishing confusion—and only an hour before even his physical appearance would reorganize, though that would no longer matter in the least.

It was time to exercise the last option—now, before the probe could bypass his cortex and again prevent him from speaking his own, fully conscious mind. He said:

"Never mind, Valkol. I'll give you what you want."

"What? By Gro, I'm not going to give you——"

"You don't have to give me anything; I'm not selling anything. You see for yourself that you can't get to the material with that machine. Nor with any other like it, I may add. But I exercise my option to turn my coat, under Guild laws; that gives me safe conduct, and that's sufficient."

"No," the Fomentor's voice said. "It is incredible—he is in no pain and has frustrated the machine; why should he yield? Besides, the secret of his resistance——"

"Hush," Valkol said. "I am moved to ask if you *are* a

vombis; doubtless, the machine would tell us that much. Mr. De Kuyl, I respect the option, but I am not convinced yet. The motive, please?"

"High Earth is not enough," Simon said. "Remember Ezra-Tse? 'The last temptation is the final treason . . . to do the right thing for the wrong reason.' I would rather deal fairly with you, and then begin the long task of becoming honest with myself. But with you only, Valkol—not the Exarchy. I sold the Green Exarch nothing."

"I see. A most interesting arrangement, I agree. What will you require?"

"Perhaps three hours to get myself unscrambled from the effects of fighting your examination. Then I'll dictate the missing material. At the moment it's quite inaccessible."

"I believe that, too," Valkol said ruefully. "Very well——"

"It is not very well," the vombis said, almost squalling. "The arrangement is a complete violation of——"

Valkol turned and looked at the creature so hard that it stopped talking of its own accord. Suddenly Simon was sure Valkol no longer needed tests to make up his mind what the Fomentor was.

"I would not expect you to understand it," Valkol said in a very soft voice indeed. "It is a matter of style."

CHAPTER ELEVEN

Simon was moved to a comfortable apartment and left alone, for well more than the three hours he had asked for. By that time, his bodily reorganization was complete, though it would take at least a day more for all the residual mental effects of the serum to vanish. When the Traitor-in-Chief finally admitted himself to the apartment, he made no attempt to disguise either his amazement or his admiration.

"The poison man! High Earth is still a world of miracles. Would it be fair to ask what you did with your, uh, over-populated associate?"

"I disposed of him," Simon said. "We have traitors enough already. There is your document; I wrote it out by hand, but you can have toposcope confirmation whenever you like now."

"As soon as my technicians master the new equipment—we shot the monster, of course, though I don't doubt the Exarch will resent it."

"When you see the rest of the material, you may not care what the Exarch thinks," Simon said. "You will find that I've brought you a high alliance—though it was Gro's own horns getting it to you."

"I had begun to suspect as much. Mr. De Kuyl—I must assume you are still he, for sanity's sake—that act of surrender was the most elegant gesture I have ever seen. That alone convinced me that you were indeed the Traitor-in-Chief of High Earth, and no other."

"Why, so I was," Simon said. "But if you will excuse me now, I think I am about to become somebody else."

With a mixture of politeness and alarm, Valkol left him. It was none too soon. He had a bad taste in his mouth which had nothing to do with his ordeals . . . and, though nobody knew better than he how empty all vengeance is, an inexpungeable memory of Jillith.

Maybe, he thought, "Justice is Love," after all—not a matter of style but of spirit. He had expected all these questions to vanish when the antidote took full hold, wiped into the past with the personalities who had done what they had done, but they would not vanish; they were himself.

He had won, but obviously he would never be of use to High Earth again.

In a way, this suited him. A man did not need the transduction serum to be divided against himself; he still had many guilts to accept, and not much left of a lifetime to do it in.

While he was waiting, perhaps he could learn to play the sareh.

The Writing of the Rat

The poem which served as a springboard for this story is cited in the text, but someone with a taste for cryptanalysis might like to puzzle out the "synthetic language" used by Hrestce (whose name is a part of the code). Clue: It came 100 per cent off a theatre marquee in Brooklyn, and it is not a foreign language—just English with some letters missing.

They had strapped the Enemy to a chair, which in John Jahnke's opinion was neither necessary nor smart, but Jahnke was only a captain (Field rank). Ugly the squat, grey-furred, sharp-toothed creatures were, certainly; and their thick bodies, well over six feet tall, were frighteningly strong. But they were also proud and intelligent. They never ran amok in a hopeless situation; that would be beneath their dignity.

The irons were going to make questioning the creature a good deal more difficult than it would have been otherwise —and that would have been difficult enough. But Jahnke was only a Field officer, and, what was worse, invalided home. Here it could hardly matter that he knew the Enemy better than any other human being alive. His opinions would be weighed against the fact that he had been invalided home from a Field where there were no battles. And the two years of captivity? A rest cure, the Home officers called them.

"Where did you take him?" he asked Major Matthews.

"Off a planet of 31 Cygni," Matthews growled, loosening his tie. "Whopping sun, a hundred fifty times as big as Sol,

51

six hundred fifty light-years from here. All alone there in a ship no bigger than a beer can."

"A scout?"

"What else? All right, he's ready." Matthews looked at the two hard-faced enlisted men behind the Enemy's chair. One of them grinned slightly. "Ask him where he's from."

The grey creature turned flat, steady eyes on Jahnke, obviously already aware that he was the interpreter. Seating, Jahnke put the question.

"Hnimesacpeo," the Enemy said.

"So far so good," Jahnke murmured. "Hnimesacpeo *tce rebo?*"

"*Tca.*"

"Well?" Matthews said.

"That's the big province in the northern hemisphere of Vega III. Thus far he's willing to be reasonable."

"The hell with that. We already knew he was Vegan. Where's his station?"

Whether or not the Enemy was Vegan was unknown, and might never be known. But there was no point in arguing that with Matthews; he already thought he knew. After a moment's struggle with the language, Jahnke tried: "*Sftir etminbi rokolny?*"

"*R-daee 'blk.*"

"Either he doesn't understand me," Jahnke said resignedly, "or he won't talk while he's in the chair. He says, 'I just told you.'"

"Try again."

"*Dirafy edic,*" Jahnke said. "*Stfir etminbu rakolna?*"

"Hnimesacpeo." The creature's eyes blinked, once. "*Ta hter o alkbëe.*"

"It's no good," Jahnke said. "He's giving me the same answer, but this time in the pejorative form—the one they use for draft animals and children. It might go better if you'd let him out of those irons."

Matthews laughed shortly. "Tell him to open up or expect trouble," he said. "The irons are only the beginning, if he's going to be stubborn."

"Sir, if you insist upon this course of action, I will appeal against it. It won't work, and it's counter to policy. We know from long experience Outside that——"

"Never mind about Outside; you're on Earth now," Matthews said harshly. "Tell him what I said."

Worse and worse. Jahnke put the message as gently as he could.

The Enemy blinked. "*Sehe et broe in icen.*"

"Well?" Matthews said.

"He says you couldn't run a maze with your shoes off," Jahnke said, with a certain grim relish. The phrase was *the* worst insult, but Matthews wouldn't know that; the literal translation could mean little to him.

Nevertheless, Matthews had brains enough to know when he was being defied. He flushed slowly. "All right," he told the toughs. "Start on him, and don't start slow."

Jahnke was abruptly wishing that he hadn't translated the insult at all, but the outcome would probably have been the same in the long run. "Sir," he said, his voice ragged, "I request your permission to leave."

"Don't be stupid. D'you think we're doing this for fun?" Since this was exactly what Jahnke thought, he was glad that the question was rhetorical. "Who'll translate when he does talk, if you're not here?"

"He won't talk."

"Yes, he will," Matthews said with relish. "And you can tell him why."

After a moment, Jahnke said stonily: "*Ocro hli antsou-tinys, fuso tizen et tobëe.*"

It was a complex message, and Jahnke was none too sure that he had got it right. The Enemy merely nodded once and looked away. There was no way of telling whether he had failed to understand, had understood and was trying to avoid betraying Jahnke, or was merely indifferent. He said: "*Seace tce ctisbe*." The phrase was formal; it might mean "thank you", but then again it might mean half a hundred equally common expressions, including "hello", "good-bye", and "time for lunch".

"Does he understand?" Matthews demanded.

"I think he does," Jahnke said. "You'll be destroying him for nothing, Major."

The prediction paid off perfectly. Two hours later, the grey creature looked at Matthews out of his remaining, lidless eye, said clearly, "*Sehe et broe in icen*," and died. He had said nothing else, though he had cried out often.

Somehow, that possible word of thanks he had given Jahnke made it worse, not better.

Jahnke went back to his quarters on shaky legs, to compose a letter of protest. He gave it up after the first paragraph. There was nobody to write to. While he had been Outside, he could have appealed to the Chief of Intelligence Operations (Field), who had been his friend as well as his immediate superior. But now he was in Novoe Washingtongrad where the CIO(F) in his remote flagship swung less weight than Home officers as far down the chain of command as Major Matthews.

It hadn't always been like that. After the discovery of the Enemy, the Field officers had commanded as much instant respect at home as Field officers always had; they were in the position of danger. But as it gradually became clear that there was going to be no war, that the Field officers were bringing home puzzles instead of victories, that the danger Outside was that of precipitating a battle rather than fighting one, the pendulum swung. Now Field officers treated the Enemy with respect, and were despised for it—while the Home officers itched for the chance to show that *they* weren't soft on the Enemy.

Matthews had had his chance, and would be itching for another.

Jahnke put down his pen and stared at the wall, feeling more than a little sick.

The grey creatures were, as it had turned out, everywhere. When the first interstellar ship had arrived in the Alpha Centauri system, there they were, running the two fertile planets from vast stony cities by means of an elaborate priesthood. The relatively infertile fourth planet they had organized as a tight autarchy of technicians, dominating a high-energy economy of scarcity. They had garrisoned several utterly barren Centaurian planets for what was vaguely called "reasons of policy", meaning that nobody knew why they had.

That had been only a foretaste. They were everywhere. No habitable planet was without them, no matter how you stretched the definition of "habitable". Their most magnificent achievement was Vega III, an Earthlike world twice the diameter of Earth and at least a century in advance of Earth technologies. But they were found, too, on the major satellite of 61 Cygni C, a "grey ghost" of a star almost small enough to be a gas-giant planet, where they lived tribal lives as cramped and penurious as those of ancient Lapland—and had the Ragnarok-like mythology to go with it.

No one could even guess how long they had known interstellar flight, or where they had come from. The hypothesis that they had originally been Vegans was shaky, based solely on the fact that Vega III was their most highly developed planet yet discovered. As for facts that argued in the opposite direction, there were more than enough, from Jahnke's point of view.

They had, for instance, a common spoken language, but every one of their civilizations had a different written language, usually irreconcilable with all the others—pictograms, phonetic systems, ideograms, hieratic shorthands, inflectional systems, tone-modulated systems, positional systems—the works. The spoken language was so complex that not even Jahnke could speak it above the primer level, for it was based on phoneme placement inside the word; in short, it was totally synthetic, derived from the Enemy's vast knowledge of information theory, and could be matched up *in part* to any written language imaginable. Thus, there was no way to tell which written language— which always abstracts from speech, and introduces new elements which have nothing to do with speech—might have been the original.

And how can you be sure you know where the Enemy's home planet is, Jahnke brooded, when you can see him still actively exploring and taking over one new system after another, for no other visible reason other than sheer acquisitiveness? How can you tell how long that process has been going on, when *no* new penetration of human beings to more distant reaches of the galaxy fails to find the grey creatures established on two or three promising planets, and nosing in on half a dozen additional cinder blocks which have nothing to recommend them but the fact that they are large enough to land upon?

"They're nothing but rats," Colonel Singh, the CIO(F), had once told Jahnke, in an excess of disgust unusual for him. "The whole damned galaxy must be overrun with them. They couldn't have evolved any civilization we ever found them in."

"They're intelligent," Jahnke had protested. "Nobody's yet measured how intelligent they are."

"Sure," Singh had said. "I'll give them that. They're more than intelligent; they're brilliant. Nevertheless, they didn't evolve any of 'their' civilizations, John. They couldn't have, because they—the civilizations—are too diversified. The Enemy maintains all of them with equal thoroughness, and equal indifference. If we could just explore some of those planets, I'll bet we'd find the bones of the original owners. How does that poem of Sandburg's go?"

His brow furrowed a moment over this apparent irrelevancy, and he quoted:

> *And the wind shifts*
> *and the dust on a doorsill shifts*
> *and even the writing of the rat footprints*
> *tells us nothing, nothing at all*
> *about the greatest city, the greatest nation*
> *where the strong men listened*
> *and the women warbled: Nothing like us ever was.*

"That's how it is," Singh added gloomily. "All these grey rats are doing is picking everybody else's cupboards. They're very good at that. They may well be picking ours before long."

That was the second theory; on the whole, it was the most popular one now. It was the theory under which a man like Matthews could torture to death a creature nine times as intelligent as he was, and with a code of customs and a set of moral standards which made Matthews look like a bushman, on the grounds that the Enemy were merely loathsome scavengers, fit only to sic cats on.

Despite his respect for Piara Singh, Jahnke could find little good to say for the rat theory, either. Both theories pointed, in the end, towards a common military goal—that of finding the Enemy's home planet and destroying it. If Vega III was the Enemy's home, then at least there was a target. If the Enemy were spreading from some other heartland, then the target still remained to be found.

But what good was that? It was military nonsense. The Enemy outnumbered humanity by millions to one. On the highly developed planets like Vega III, the Enemy commanded weapons compared to which humanity's best were only torches to be waved in the face of the inevitable night.

The first moment of open warfare would be the end of humanity.

So far, the grey creatures and humanity were not at war. But the time of the explosion was drawing closer. Jahnke did not really think that the Enemy could be still in ignorance of Earth's practice of picking up its lone scouts for questioning; the Enemy's resources were too great. It was his private theory, shared by Piara Singh, that the Enemy was content to let its scouts be questioned, as long as they were set free unharmed afterwards. After all, the Enemy had once picked up Jahnke under the same circumstances and for the same purpose; it was for that reason that he knew their language better than any other human being; he had lived among them for two years.

But if Matthews' Inquisition methods represented a new and general policy towards these occasional captives, the Enemy would not let that policy go unprotested. The grey creatures were very proud. Jahnke knew that, for they had expected no less pride of him.

And what would happen when one of the Enemy's scouts came nosing acquisitively, at long last, into the Solar system of Earth—even around so cold, dark and useless a world as the satellite of Proserpine, far beyond Pluto? Earth had no use for that rockball, but it would never let the "rats" have it, all the same. Of course, thus far the grey tide had spared the Sol system, but that couldn't last forever. The grey tide had, after all, spared nothing else.

The phone rang insistently, jarring Jahnke out of his bitter reverie. He picked it up.

"Captain Jahnke? One moment, please. Colonel Singh calling."

Jahnke clung to the phone in a state of numb shock, uncertain whether to be delighted or appalled. What could Piara Singh be doing here, out of the high, free emptiness of Outside? Had he been invalided home again, too, or had some failure—

"John? How are you? This is Singh. I called the moment I got in."

"Hello, Colonel, I'm astonished, and pleased. But what——"

"I know what you're thinking," the CIO(F) said rapidly. His voice was high with suppressed eagerness; Jahnke had never heard him sound so young before. "I'm home on my own initiative, on special orders I wormed out of old Wu himself. I brought a prisoner with me—and John, listen, he's the most important prisoner we've ever taken. He told me his name."

"No! They never do. It's against the rules."

"But he did," Singh said, almost bubbling. "It's Hrestce, and in the language it means 'compromise', isn't that right? I think he was deliberately sent to us with a message. That's why I came home. The key to the whole problem seems to be in his hands, and he obviously wants to talk. I have to have you to listen to him and tell me what it means."

Jahnke's heart tried to rise and sink at the same time, enclosing his whole chest in an awful vise of apprehension. "All right," he said faintly. "Did you notify CIO? Here in Novoe Washingtongrad, I mean?"

"Oh, of course," Singh said. His enthusiasm seemed to be about to burst the telephone handset—and small wonder, after all the setbacks which had made up his career Outside. "They recognized how important this is right away. They've assigned their best interrogation man to me, a Major Matthews. I don't doubt that he's good, but we'll need you first. If you can get here for a preliminary talk with Hrestce——"

"I can get there," Jahnke said tensely. "But don't let *anyone* else talk to him before I do. This Matthews is dangerous. If he calls before I arrive, stall him. Where are you calling from?"

"At home, on the Kattegat," Singh said. "I have three weeks' leave. You know the place, don't you? You can reach it in an hour, if you can catch a rocket right away. I can keep Hrestce in my jurisdiction for you that long easily. Nobody but you and the CIO knows he's here."

"Don't even let CIO to him until I get there. I'll see you in an hour."

"Right, John. Good-bye."

"*Seace tce ctisbe.*"

"Yes—how does it go? *Tca.*"

"*Tce; tca.*"

Trembling with excitement and urgency, Jahnke got the rest of his mussed uniform off, clambered into mufti, and packed his equipment: a tape recorder, two dictionaries compiled by himself, a set of frequency tables for the Enemy language which he had not yet completed, and a toothbrush. At the last moment, he remembered to take his officer's I.D. card, and money to buy his rocket ticket. Now. All ready.

He opened the door to go out.

Matthews was there. His feet were wide apart, his hands locked behind his back, his brow thrust forward. He looked like a lowering, small-scale copy of the Colossus of Rhodes.

"Morning, Captain Jahnke," Matthews said, with a slight and nasty smile. "Going somewhere? The Kattegat, maybe?"

The soldiers behind Matthews, those same two wooden-faced toughs, helped him wait for Jahnke's answer.

After a moment of sickening doubt, Jahnke went back into his quarters, into the kitchen, out of Matthews' sight. He found the bottle of cloudy ammonia his batman used for scrubbing his floors, and shook it until it was full of foam. Then he went back into the front room and threw the bottle as hard as he could into the corridor. It seemed to explode like a bomb.

He had to kick one soldier who made it through the fumes into the front room; but he got away over the man's body, his eyes streaming. Now all he had to do was to make it to Singh before Matthews did.

It would be a near thing. Temporarily, at least, time was on his side, Jahnke was pretty sure. Piara Singh's Kattegat home was a retreat, quite possibly unlisted among the addresses the government had for him; Jahnke had learned

60

of it only through a few moments of nostalgia in which the colonel had indulged over a drink. If so, Matthews would have a difficult time searching the shores of the strait for it, and might think only very belatedly of looking in the wildest part of Jutland.

Also in Jahnke's favour was the fact that Matthews was, after all, only a major. The man whose leave he had to plan on invading was a full colonel, even though only a despised Field officer—and the despite in which Field officers were held was in itself only a symptom of the Home officers' guilt at being Home officers. Matthews would probably pause to collect considerable official backing before venturing further.

All this was logical, but Jahnke knew Matthews too well to be comforted by it.

He got a liner direct to Copenhagen, which cut down his transit time considerably. After that, there was only the complicated business of getting off the islands on to the peninsula, and thence north to Alborg. Colonel Singh had a car waiting for him there, which took him direct to the door of the lodge.

"An hour and a half," Singh said, shaking hands. "That was good time."

"The best. Glad to see you, sir. We're going to have to move fast, I'm afraid; we're not safe even here. This bird Matthews is a dedicated sadist. Do you remember the prisoner that was sent home with me? Well, Matthews tortured him to death just yesterday, trying to get routine information out of him. He'll do the same with your captive if he gets his hands on him. He knows I'm here, of course. Either my telephone wire was tapped—they all are, I suppose—or he knew that you'd call me as soon as the news trickled down to him at CIO."

An expression of revulsion totally transformed Colonel Singh's lean brown face for a moment, but he said decisively: "So it's come to that; they must be cut off from the real situation Outside almost entirely, and it's their own fault. Well, I know what we can do. I have a private plane here, and my pilot is the very best. We'll just take ourselves upstairs and defy this Matthews to get us down again until we're good and ready."

"Where are we going?" Jahnke asked.

"I don't know at the moment, and it doesn't matter. There are a lot of places to hide inside a thousand-mile radius where Matthews wouldn't think of looking for us, if we *have* to hide. But I think I can pull his teeth through channels before it comes to that. Come on, better meet the prisoner."

He led the way into the next room. The prisoner was looking at a book which, Jahnke could see as he put it aside, was mostly mathematics. He was an unusually big specimen even for an Enemy, with enormous shoulders and arms, a deep chest, and a brow which gave him an expression of permanent ferocity; he looked as though he could have torn Jahnke and the colonel to pieces without the slightest effort, as indeed he probably could.

"Hrestce, John Jahnke," Colonel Singh said.

"*Seace tce ctisbe*," Jahnke said.

"*Tce*." Hrestce held out his hand, and Jahnke took it somewhat nervously. Then, drawing a deep breath, he quickly outlined the situation, pulling no punches. When he got to the part about the death of Matthews' prisoner, Hrestce only nodded; when Jahnke proposed that they leave, he nodded again; that was all.

They were aloft in ten minutes. The pilot took them west, towards the blasted remains of the British Isles; they had suffered heavily in the abortive Third World War, and nobody flew over them by preference, or patrolled the air there—there was no territory left worth patrolling.

In the cabin of the plane, Jahnke started his tape recorder and got out his manuscript dictionary. With Hrestce's first words, however, it became apparent that he wasn't going to need the dictionary. The Enemy spoke simply, though with great dignity, and quickly found the speech rate which was comfortable for Jahnke. When he spoke to Singh, he slowed down even more; he seemed already aware that Singh's command of the language did not extend to high-order abstractions or subtle constructions.

"I am an emissary, as Colonel Singh surmised," Hrestce said. "My mission is to appraise you of the search my people have been conducting, and to take such further steps as your reaction dictates. By 'you', of course, I mean mankind."

"What is the search?" Jahnke said.

"First I must explain some other matters," Hrestce said. "You have some incomplete truths about us which should be completed now. You know that we occupy many dissimilar civilizations; you suspect that they are not ours, and that the original owners are gone. That is true. You think you have never seen our home culture. That is also true; our planet of origin is far out on the end of this spiral arm of the galaxy, from which we have been working our way inward towards the centre. You think we have usurped the original owners of these cultures. That is not true. We have another function. We are custodians."

"Custodians?" Singh said. "Custodians of cultures?"

"Of cultures, of entire ecologies. That is the role which has been thrust upon us. When we first mastered interstellar flight, sometime in the prehistory of your race, we found these empty planets by the hundreds. We found only a few inhabited ones, which I will describe in a moment.

"The research which followed was tedious, and I shall do no more than describe its results. Briefly, there is a race in this galaxy *which is practising slavery on an incredible scale*. We know who they are, for we have encountered several of their slave planets, but they fight ferociously and without quarter, so that we have been unable to find out where they came from, or why they want so many billions and billions of slaves. Their usual practice, however, is to evacuate a planet entirely; there is evidence of resistance on all the empty worlds, but the battles and losses were never large—evidently the slavers utterly overwhelmed them. The bones we find never account for more than a tenth of the total population of the planet, usually much less. Yet the people are gone, leaving nothing behind but their effects, which the raiders seldom bother to loot.

"We do not know how many of those conquered and enslaved races are still alive. Under the circumstances, we have chosen to maintain each culture on its own terms, in the hope that at least some of them may be re-possessed by their owners in the future, as we have already turned back the liberated worlds. It is for that reason that we have evolved this synthetic language, which is adaptable to any culture and carries the implicit assumptions of none." The grey creature paused, and the expression which crossed his face was something like a fleeting smile. "After speaking it for so many millennia, we find we rather like it; some of us are doing creative work in it."

"I like it very well," Jahnke said. "It's highly flexible; I should think it might make a good medium for poetry."

"There you make a statement with import for your race," Hrestce said. The smile, if that was what it had been, was gone without a trace. "It was your poetry, to some extent, that deterred us from wiping you all out at once, as we have the power to do. For I must tell you plainly now that *you are an outpost of the slavers we are seeking.*"

Jahnke had seen it coming, if only hazily; but it hurt, all the same.

"We were in doubt at first; though the physical form is the same, your obvious creativity and your frequent flashes of sanity and decency seemed anomalous. Also, there seemed to be evidence that you had evolved on this planet. Further investigation disposed of that point, however; of all your presumptive ancestors, only the half-simian, stone-throwing culture of South Africa is indigenous to Earth. All the others you brought with you from other planets—as slaves—and the stone throwers you wiped out as being of too little intelligence to be useful. The Cro-Magnons, for example, were the descendants of the race of Vega III; there is no doubt whatever about it."

There was a long silence in the gently circling plane. At last Jahnke said hollowly: "What now? Since you have decided not to wipe us out——"

"There is the heart of the question," Hrestce said. "You have been cut off from the moral imbeciles who spawned you for a long time, and during that time you have changed. Your race still reverts to the parent type now and then: You throw up an Alexander, a Khan, a Napoleon, a Hitler, a Stalin, a McCarthy—or a Matthews. But plainly, these are now subhuman types, and will become ever more rare with time.

"We have been hunting for the main body of these slavers for a long time. They have crimes beyond number to answer for. They may have changed greatly in twenty-five thousand years, as you have changed; if so, we will be gratified. If they have not changed, we are prepared to destroy them down to the last mad creature."

Hrestce paused and looked at the two men with sombre ferocity.

"The task is enormous," he said, "because of the care-taking responsibilities that go with it. We would share it with someone if we could. We have decided to ask you if you would so share it. The growth you have undergone is staggering; it shows potentialities which we believe are greater than ours."

A long sigh exploded from Singh; evidently, he had been holding his breath longer than he himself had realized. "So all the time you were the rat terriers, and *we* were the rats," he said. "Matthews fits the description, all right. When I get through with him, he's going to be breaking rocks."

As for Jahnke, he would have found it hard to say whether he was awed or elated, for both emotions had overwhelmed him at once. Matthews and his ilk were certainly through; the Field officers had won, after all; they had brought home not only the bacon, but the laurel wreath—not a bloody victory to be lived down, but a mighty standard to be followed.

"Can we accept?" Jahnke whispered at last.

The colonel shook his head. "There's only one man that can," he said, his own voice just barely audible above the drone of the plane. "But he'll listen to us now—and I think I know what the answer will be."

He stood shakily and went forward to the door of the control cubby. "West as she goes," he told the pilot huskily. "For Novoe Washingtongrad. And get me the Secretary-General on the radio—direct."

"Yes, sir."

Piara Singh closed the door and came back. While the plane turned over the dark Atlantic, the three rat terriers put their heads together.

In some cupboard towards the centre of the galaxy, the writing of the rat was waiting to be read.

And Some Were Savages

The title of this story is not intended to convey any connection with that of Lester del Rey's first collection of short stories, *And Some Were Human*; the resemblance is pure accident. The story was written around a magazine cover which showed a group of aliens dancing around a grounded spaceship, brandishing crossbows. In tackling such a chore, the first thing the writer must do is question the artist's assumptions, which are usually as obvious as a cartoon; so in this case I first had to ask myself, "Which are the savages?"

The French, as is well known, can cook, and so can the Italians, who taught them how. The Germans can cook, and so can the Scandinavians and the Dutch; Greek cooking is good if you like chervil, and Armenian if you can endure lamb fat and honey; Spanish cooking is excellent if your Spaniard can find something to cook, and the same goes for most Asiatic cuisines; and so on, thank goodness.

The cook aboard the U.N.S.S. *Brock Chisholm*, though, was an Englishman. He boiled everything. Sometimes for chow you got the things themselves, deeply jacketed in mosquito netting; and sometimes, instead, you got the steam condensed off them, garnished with scraps of limp lettuce which had turned black with age. The latter was sometimes called soup, and sometimes called tea.

This is just one of the hazards—one of the more usual ones—of interstellar pioneering; and though I've heard that things have gotten a little softer in recent years, I can't say that I've seen any signs of it. Even aboard the *Chisholm*, I was sometimes accused of making a god of my stomach, even by Captain Motlow; which was plainly unfair, considering the quantities of steamed-shoes-in-muslin which I'd gnawed at without complaint during the first few months of the trip.

All the same, I did my best to stay on my dignity, as is expected of every officer and gentleman commissioned by act of the General Assembly.

"An army marches on its stomach," I pointed out, "and I'm supposed to be a fighting man. I don't mind servicing my own arms, or that my batman doesn't seem to know how to press a uniform, or even having to baby-tend Dr. Roche. All that's part of the normal grab bag you get in the field. But——"

"Yah-huh," Captain Motlow said. He was a tall, narrow man, and except for his battleship prow of a chin, looked as though he were leather himself. "You're also supposed to be an astrogator, Hans. Get your mind off sauerbraten and on to the problem at hand, will you?"

I looked at the planet on the screens and made a slight correction for the third moon—a tiny, jagged mass of dense rock with a retrograde movement and high eccentricity, very hard to allow for without longer observation time than we'd had up to now. Inevitably, it reminded me of something.

"I've got the problem in hand," I said stiffly, pointing to the tab board showing my figures in glowing characters. He swivelled around in his chair to look up at them. "And don't think it was easy. How long is the *Chisholm* going to last with an astrogator who hasn't had any B vitamins since he left Earth, except what I wangled out of Doc Bixby's stores? Astrogation demands steady nerves—and that hunk of rock we had last night for dinner was no more a sauerbraten than I am."

"Don't tempt me, Lieutenant Pfeiffer," Captain Motlow

said. "We may hit cannibalism enough down below. If you're *damn* sure we can put the *Chisholm* into this orbit, we'll go have our meeting with Dr. Roche. Between meals, we've got work to do."

"Certainly, I'm sure," I said. Motlow nodded and turned back to push the "do-so" button. The figures vanished from the tab board into the banks, and for a while the *Chisholm* groaned and heaved as she was pushed into the orbit around our goal. That's one thing I can say for Motlow: when I told him the figures were right, he trusted me. He never had any reason to be sorry for it, and neither has any other captain.

All the same, he's also far from the only captain to give me the impression that field-commissioned officers *like* boiled shoes.

Dr. Armand Roche was another of my crosses aboard the *Chisholm*, but also so ordinary a feature of any U.N.R.R.A. crash-rescue mission in deep space that I could hardly complain about him. Crash rescue, after all, is a general cross mankind bears—and may have to bear for some centuries yet—in payment for the poor forethought the first interstellar explorers exercised in the practice of a science called gnotobiosis.

Maybe they couldn't be blamed for that, since they had never heard of the term. It is the science of living a totally germ-free life; in other words, the most extreme form of sanitation and public health imaginable. In the first days of space travel, nobody suspected that it would eventually have to come to that. The builders of the first unmanned rockets did think to sterilize their missiles as best they could, and in fact the proposition that it would be unwise (and scientifically confusing) to contaminate other planets with Earthly life was embodied in several international agreements. But nobody thought of man himself as a contaminant until far too late.

"There were a few harbingers," Dr. Roche was telling the quiet group in the officers' mess. He was a smallish, bland-faced, rumpled man, but he spoke with considerable passion when he saw any occasion to. "In fact, the very term 'gnotobiosis' goes back to the March 1959 issue of the *World Medical Journal*—one of the many important ideas the U.N. was spawning hand over fist in those days, to the total indifference of the world at large. Even then, somebody saw that the responsibility for introducing the TB germ, the rabies virus, the anthrax spore, the encephalitis virus to a virgin planet would be very heavy."

"I don't see why," said Sergeant Lea, the blond, loose-jointed Marine squad leader. "Everybody knows that human beings couldn't possibly catch an alien disease, or aliens catch a human one. Their body chemistries are too different."

"That's one of those things that 'everybody knows' that's wrong," Dr. Roche said, "and I see by your expression that you're quite aware of it; thanks for the leading question. I chose my examples specifically to cover that point. All the diseases I mentioned are zoonoses—that is, diseases which circulate very freely between many different types of creatures, even on Earth. Rabies will attack virtually every kind of warm-blooded animal, and pass from one phylum to another at a scratch. Most serious parasitic diseases, like bilharziasis or malaria, are transmitted through snails, armadillos, kissing bugs, goats: you name the critter and I'll pop up with a zoonosis to go with it. Diseases of man are caused by bacteria, fungi, protozoa, viruses, worms, fish, flowering plants, and so on. And diseases of these creatures are caused by man."

"I never heard of a man making a plant sick," said a very young Marine private named Oberholzer.

"Then you have never met a mimosa, to name only one of a whole catalogue of examples. And even micro-organisms harmless on Earth might well prove dangerous on

70

other soil, or in other races—which in fact is what *has* happened over and over again, and why we are in orbit around this planet now."

"We gave them measles?"

"Not funny," Dr. Roche said. "European explorers introduced measles into the Polynesian Islands, which had never known it before, and it turned out to be a massively fatal disease—for a non-immune population of adults. Columbus' expedition was probably the importer of syphilis from the West Indies into Europe, and for two centuries thereafter it cut Europeans down as rapidly and surely as gangrene; its later, chronic form didn't become characteristic of the disease until the antibodies against the organism were circulating through the population of Europe as a whole. It's possible that only one single man in Columbus' fleet was responsible for that vast epidemic mortality, and for the many additional centuries of suffering and loss and disgrace that followed before cures were found. It's a hideous kind of risk to take, but the first interstellar explorers, who should have known better, also took it—and the price is still being paid. This expedition of ours is part of that price."

"So if I sneeze on patrol," Oberholzer said, "I get KP?"

Lea glared at him. "No," he said, "you get shot. Shaddup and listen."

Lea's pique was understandable. His leading question had been designed to remind Oberholzer and any other green hands like him that we all, Dr. Roche included, had been brought up on birth farms, and so give Roche just the opening he needed to abort such a line of questioning as Oberholzer was following. The sergeant did not take kindly to the failure of his rudimentary essay into dialectics.

Roche, however, explained patiently. The Earth had not been sterilized yet, and probably never would be; even now, nobody really warmed to the idea of disrupting the grand ecology of the whole home planet simply for the protection of worlds and races many light-years away, or even still undiscovered. But the intermediate step was a fact, as Roche should not have needed to point out.

For instance, there was not a pig in any herd on Earth any more, nor had there been for centuries, who was not certified to be specific-pathogen-free, by virtue of having been born along with the rest of his litter by radical hysterectomy and raised on the bottle. And there was not a man aboard the *Chisholm*, or anywhere else in space today, who had not been from his mother's womb untimely ripp'd into a totally germ-free environment—which he still carried inside his body, and which still carried him in his ship.

On the other hand, maybe I was expecting too much of a private of Marines on his first crash-rescue mission (or, for all I knew, his first mission of any kind). As I've noted, the astrogator is traditionally one of the two officers on a crash-rescue ship who are assigned to provide intellectual companionship to the U.N.R.R.A. civilian in charge, the other being the ship's surgeon. The assumption behind the tradition seems to be that any other Giant Brains who might be aboard would be too busy. Well, there was some justice in that, for while an astrogator is very busy indeed when he's busy at all, it's in the nature of the job to be concentrated at the opposite ends of a trip, leaving a long dead space in between. I get a lot of reading done that way: poetry, mostly. And doctoring, of course, is a notoriously off-again on-again proposition, especially with a population as small as a ship's crew to look after, and nary a germ anywhere aboard (ideally, at least).

Hence though I had never heard Roche's speech before, I had heard many like it. Up to this point I could have given it myself, and probably played a fair game of chess at the same time. Now, however, he was getting to the part that only he could testify to: the nature of the *specific* situation beneath us on this mission.

"The first explorers who landed here called the planet Savannah, though maybe 'Tundra' or 'Veldt' would have been more suitable," he was saying. "It's a dense, high-gravity world about seven thousand miles in diameter. It consists mostly of broad, grassy plains, broken here and there by volcanic ranges and some rather small oceans.

"However, they didn't explore it thoroughly, for reasons I'll get to in a moment. They made contact with the natives very early, and described them as savages but friendly. No xenologist would agree that they're savages, not from the descriptions we have. They are hunters primarily, but they also herd, and raise crops. They weave, and build boats, and navigate by the stars. They are also metalworkers, technically very ingenious, but limited by the fact that they lack the energy sources to do really large-scale, high-temperature smelting and forging, thus far.

"They have a family system, and a system of small nations or family tribes, and a certain amount of internecine warfare in bad years. Both of these facts contributed to the downfall of the first expedition to Savannah. The Earthmen inadvertently infected these initially friendly people with a very common Earthly disease which turned out to be virulently deadly to the males of the native population. The females are not immune, but are naturally far more resistant.

"This plague played hob with the native families, and this in turn began to threaten old alliances and balances of power between the tribes, as well as the division of labour within the tribes themselves. The natives were quick to associate it with their strange visitors, and one night, without the slightest warning, they attacked the landing camp. Very few of the landing party got away alive—and there were no wounded among them."

"Poisoned darts?" Sergeant Lea said interestedly.

"No," Dr. Roche returned grimly. "Quarrels."

Lea looked puzzled.

"Those are crossbow bolts," Roche explained. "In this case, heavy metal ones, launched with such high velocity that they can kill a man no matter where they hit him, through shock alone. I bring this up so you'll know in advance that full battle dress is going to be of dubious value at best. We are going to have to plan in such a way that nobody gets hit—and *without* killing or injuring so much as one native. Just how we're going to manage that, I'll have to leave up to you."

Lea shrugged. He was used to being handed the hard ones.

"All right. Now what we *want* to do isn't quite as complicated. We need to capture a number of natives with status among their fellows—warriors will doubtless do; learn more of their language; win their confidence; and explain to them that we have a cure. And we will have to convince them that they must abandon their first natural desire, which will be to give the antivirus to their sick warriors and kings. The stuff won't work with them; they're doomed. Instead, it will have to be given to expectant mothers, exclusively."

"That's going to take a lot of convincing," Captain Motlow said.

"Agreed. But that's one of the main reasons why I'm here. Nor is that all. There's a time limit. Unlike human beings, the natives here have a fixed mating season, so all their babies go to term at once, practically speaking. We got here as fast as we could once we learned the story, but we are right on the edge of the whelping season now. If we don't get most of this generation of pregnant females injected—for which native help is imperative; we haven't the manpower to do it ourselves—the race will be wiped out. The male children will die in infancy, and that will be that.

"That's all I know about the situation, and all anybody knows. So I have to conclude: gentlemen, you must take it from there."

A stocky, middle-aged man with completely white hair—Clyde Bixby, the ship's surgeon—raised his hand. "One fact

I think you skipped, Doctor," he said. "And I think it's interesting in this context. Why not tell the assembled company what the plague was?"

"Oh. Sure," Dr. Roche said. "It was tobacco mosaic."

Nobody but Doc Bixby seemed to believe him at first, and after all, Bixby had already had the benefit of the explanation—or as much of it as Dr. Roche knew. But a lot of them ground out their cigarettes like they were crushing poisonous snakes, all the same. Roche grinned.

"Don't worry," he said. "One reason tobacco mosaic is so abundant on Earth is because it's harmless to humans. And as far as tobacco growers are concerned, it can be controlled in the fields—not cured, but controlled—by streptomycin spraying."

"A curious thing in itself," Doc Bixby put in. "Streptomycin is no good at all against any other virus."

"Well, it's no more than indifferently good against mosaic, either," Dr. Roche emphasized. "But that's not important now. The point is: For the tobacco plant, mosaic is one of the most highly infectious diseases man has ever studied. The virus isn't a tiny but relatively complex organism, as most viruses that attack man and other animals are. Instead, it's a simple chemical compound. You can prepare it in crystal form as easily as you'd make rock salt or rock candy. It isn't alive, not until it gets into the plant cell; the life it leads thereafter is entirely 'borrowed' from the host. And it's simple enough chemically so that most reagents—physical or chemical—don't destroy its integrity.

"The result is that if you walk into a greenhouse where tobacco is growing, and you're smoking a cigarette which was made from the leaf of a plant that had had mosaic, most of the growing plants will come down with the disease. They literally contract it from the smoke. And that seems to be exactly what the Savannahans did. They picked it up from cigarettes the first explorers offered them."

"As a peace pipe, maybe?" Bixby speculated.

"Maybe. If so, it's a great fat example of what a mess you can make by pushing an analogy too far."

"But why were they susceptible in the first place?" I asked.

Roche spread his hands. "God knows, Hans. It's just lucky for them that we know how the virus operates. It heads right for the chromosomes during cell division, and alters a set of genes in such a way that the daughter cells become susceptible to the disease in its overt, or 'clinical', phase. That's why it kills off the offspring so much faster than it does the adult generation: because cell division goes on so much faster in infants."

"It sure does," Doc Bixby said. "In humans, the average is ten complete replacements of all the cells in the body per lifetime—and eight of those take place between conception and the age of two."

"Well, we can denature this virus relatively simply," Dr. Roche said. "Lucky for the Savannahans that we can—*if we can do it in time*. I think we'd better get down to business."

Sergeant Lea's expression, which had begun to look like that of an insecurely tethered balloon, turned flinty with an almost audible clink.

We came down on Savannah that night in the ship's gig, it being impossible to land the *Chisholm* on this planet or any planet. I was aboard, because it was part of my job to pilot the cranky, graceless, ungrateful landing craft. Furthermore, I had to fly her in complete blackness over terrain I knew only in vaguely general terms; and I was under orders to land her silently, which is almost impossible to do with a vessel driven solely by two rockets (for space) and two ramjets (for air).

Sure, I wasn't going to use the rockets for landing, and I could cut the athodydes; but when I did that the gig dropped like a skimming stone. Though she was primarily an aircraft, she had very little lifting area, and could be

76

said to glide only by courtesy (which certainly would be extended only by somebody watching her safely through binoculars).

Nevertheless, I gave it a brave try. I wrestled her through the blackness to what seemed by the instruments to be about fifty feet above the expanse of veldt Sergeant Lea had chosen. Then I poured on enough throttle to get her well beyond aerodynamic flying speed, and cut her out, hoping to edge her still lower to the ground before she stalled out.

It worked, but it was rough. We were closer to the ground than I'd estimated, so we stalled out from what must have been no more than a few inches. Engines or no engines, it was *not* quiet—we could hear the screech of wet grass bursting into steam under the skids, right through both layers of hull.

I never touched the brakes. I didn't want us to come to a stop until we were as far away as possible from the echoes of that scream. I hate hot landings. By the time the gig actually lurched to a stop, we were twenty miles away from where we'd planned to be, and every face on board was livid—mine most of all.

I don't mind being a pioneer, exactly, but I hope someday they'll give me a softer horse. I wasn't aware of having said so aloud, but I must have, for behind me Sergeant Lea said sourly:

"The next time I have to land on a high-gravity planet, I hope they give *me* a thinner pilot."

I maintained a dignified, commissioned-officer's silence. Shortly I heard the faint rattle of gear behind me as the Marines unstrapped themselves, and checked their battle dress. By this time I judged myself to be enough over the shakes to risk checking my own suit, helmet, air supply, and flamer, and then the critical little device which was to be the trigger of our trap—if the trap worked. The trigger seemed to be in good order, and so did the relay assembly on my control board which was supposed to respond to it.

It was Lea's job to make sure that the answering action was appropriate, and I knew I could trust him for that.

"All right, Lieutenant Pfeiffer?"

"Looks all right. Let's go."

I doused all the lights, sealed myself up, and followed the Marine squad out the airlock and down into the tall grass. I couldn't resist looking up. The sky was a deep violet, in which the stars twinkled like lightning bugs—the kind of sight you don't often enjoy in a spaceman's life. I had a notion that if I stayed here long enough to become light-adapted, I might even manage to make out a few of the simpler and more banal constellations. From here, for instance, you ought to be able to make out Orion, and begin to catch distorted hints of the constellation the Sun belongs to from far away, called the Parrot. Only a computer can analyse out constellations in space; the eye can see nothing but the always visible stars, clouds and clouds of them, glaring and motionless. . . .

However, I had better sense than to daydream long on office time. I set the airlock to cycling, and touched my helmet to the closed outer seal to listen for the muted groan of the flamers. It came through right on time, a noise half-way between a low bull-fiddle note and that of a motor trying to start. Satisfied, more or less, I plodded away through the extremely tall grass.

It was lonely here. My radar sweeper kept me posted on where the gig was, and where I was supposed to go from there; but I was not going to have any company, because I was to be only one unit of a very wide circle, and the Marines were already fanning out and away from me to take up their own posts on that perimeter.

Possibly I was already being stalked, too. If so, the radar would never let me know about it, as long as the stalker kept himself bent low in the sea of grass. Above, the violet sky arched and burned. It was moonless, we had been careful enough about our timing to ensure that; but there were no clouds, either. If the natives had sharp eyes, as hunters had to have, they might well see the glints of starlight on my helmet, or even on the shoulders of my suit. And I was very aware of my weight. Every step was elephantine. I had to admit to the alien night that I was not really in very good shape for a fighting man, hard though I tried to blame it all on the 1·8 Gee field.

And my flamer was locked to my suit. We were under no circumstances to use them to defend ourselves, and couldn't have gotten them unlocked in time to disobey the order. They were only for afterwards, in case the flaming circuit inside the airlock had been knocked out for some reason. As weapons, they were as useless tonight as a tightly laced boot.

After at least a thousand million increasingly ponderous, sweating steps, the PPI scope told me I had walked out the prescribed two and a half miles. I switched to rebroadcast, and got the picture as the gig saw it. My set had a few pips that might have been Marines, but it was impossible for my suit sweeper to see all around the circle. On repeat from the gig, the scope showed several men still coming into line on the far side, which gratified me for no reason I could pin down.

They straggled in, and then each pip in the circle turned red, one by one, showing me that they too were now getting the rebroadcast and, hence, were aware of where all the rest of us were. I ran a nose count: . . . ten, eleven, and twelve, counting me. Okay.

So far, no sign of savages. But they too were present and accounted for. The radar didn't show them, and neither by eye nor by sniperscope could I see anything more than the night and the waves going over the grass. But Dr. Roche had assured us that they would be there—and games theory penetrates the strategic night far better than any sensing instrument, alive or dead.

I cut out of the rebroadcast and cut in again, making my

own pip blink green for a moment. At once, all eleven other pips went green and stayed that way. They had seen the warning.

It was time for human vision.

I snapped shut the lock switch on my little device. The gig came glaring into blue-white, almost intolerable existence in the middle of our circle. A triplet of star shells stitched across the sky above her. I could almost read the hateful legend on her side.

And there were the savages.

For those crucial three seconds they sat transfixed on their six-legged mounts, knees clenched across pommels, disproportionately long spines stiff, long bald heads thrown back, staring up at the star shells. The hairy, brown, cruelly beaked creatures they were sitting on stared too, stretching out necks as long as those of camels.

There were four of them inside my part of the circle. One was so near that I could even see that his skin, though bright yellow-red predominantly, had a faint greenish cast. He was barefoot, but he was wearing rough cloth, and a metallic belt with clear shadowings of totemistic designs worked into it.

Of course, I can't vouch for the veracity of the colours I saw. Star-shell light is lurid and chemical; and I had been in darkness a long time before it burst over all this. But the colours, true or not, were vivid after long blackness.

I also saw the crossbow, loaded and cocked; and the quiver full of quarrels. If he were to turn and see me, hardly ten yards away from him, and as rooted to the ground as a melting snowman—

But the shells dimmed and fell, leaving behind rapidly fading trails which twisted and flowed almost horizontally into the jetstream aloft before they vanished. Precisely three seconds later, all the gig's searchlights went on, right here on the ground.

The long, rounded heads snapped down. At the same time the beasts screamed and leapt so high that they seemed all at once to be flying.

They charged the gig without a moment's hesitation. They were a wild and impossibly moving sight. At a full gallop the llama-like hexapods seemed to soar over the grass almost all the way, passing above the veldt in long graceful undulations like flurries of night wind. The savages bestrode them easily, just over the beasts' middle pelvis, high-stirruped but without reins, and indeed far too far from the slashing, screaming heads to make reins even possible—rode so easily that in silhouette, savage and beast flowed into one teratological myth, like Siamese-twin centaurs. The front horse-and-head was for leaping and screaming. The back one, merged with it, was for winding and firing the arablast. The leaping was beautiful; the screaming was fearful—and the bowmen didn't miss.

One of the port lights went out, and then the other. For a few seconds I could see the two farthest riders on my side in the glow of one of the starboard lamps, and then that was gone too. They had a little more trouble with the sweep searchlight atop the gig, which was just forward of the vertical stabilizer and slightly protected both by its motion and by the curve of the fuselage. But they got it, and they got it the hard way: They shot at its junction with the hull every time it looked away from one or another of them, and after that had jammed it to a standstill, one more quarrel at point-blank range blinded it for good.

Blackness. Worse than blackness, for it was swimming with amoeboid purple after-images.

I stood where I was, certain that by now I had sunk into the soil almost up to my waist. After I thought I might be able to see the PPI scope again, I tried to get a rebroadcast from the gig, though I was pretty sure most of the savages would now be protected from that kind of spotting by being in the lee of the hull. But as it turned out, I didn't even get a scanning sweep. Evidently they had shot off the antennae, too, the instant they had gotten close enough to see that they rotated. If it moves, shoot it!

So I waited. There was nothing else to do. Roche had been right thus far, in general at least, and so the next step was to be dictated strictly by the clock. After the fury and beauty of the attack, this second wait seemed to go on forever. I have been in ground battles before, battles in which I was in more danger and had more to do, battles in which I had to defend myself, and did; but I have never seen anything like that attack on Savannah, and never hope to again.

Inside one of the purple splotches, I saw the word CONESTOGA in wavering white letters. It made me grind my teeth. As Roche had said, there was such a thing as pushing an analogy too far. But the worst of it was, nobody on *this* mission had so pushed it. It had just been somebody else's feeble joke—and it turned out to be horribly, entirely appropriate.

My clock went out. Time to start slogging back. It took an eternity, but at least I gradually got back my sight of the stars. At half a mile away from the gig, I reluctantly had to give that up again. I touched the gadget, and the gig responded with a fourth star shell.

Most of the beasts were loose and grazing. There were two savages on guard outside the gig, holding their mounts, one at her needle nose, the other by the airlock. At this distance Sergeant Lea's men had no trouble gassing them both. When I touched the gadget still a third time, the gig let loose with a twenty-decibel, wavering honk which catapulted the remaining hexapods for the horizon as though they had never been domesticated at all. I resented it, a little. Dammit, couldn't Roche have been a *little* bit wrong?

But he wasn't, not then. The other six savages were inside the gig, as soundly gassed at my signal as their two guards

had been by the Marines' grenades. They had been wrecking
things, but hadn't had time to get past the fragile, hyper-
active dummies Roche had had us set up for them to wreck.
Nor had they gotten beyond the dummy chamber into the
sterile areas of the ship, where the business is conducted.
We stacked them right there according to directions and
sealed them in. Then we flamed each other off and sealed
ourselves in.

It didn't do us much good. There were no less than sixty-
four crossbow-bolt heads sticking through the inner wall of
the gig. Not one savage could have missed it more than
twice. We seared them off and slapped patches over the
remains of the holes, but we had to go back to the *Chisholm*
inside our suits. The gig was airtight again; but gnoto-
biotically, she had been breached, and thoroughly.

Roche had her destroyed, except for the dummy chamber
where the sleeping savages were, before he would let any
one of us back into the *Chisholm* and again, I think he had
planned all along to do exactly that. It was all right with
me; I hated the CONESTOGA. The trouble is, I can't
forget her—or, rather, I can't forget her name. It's stupid
to have the memory of a great affair marred by something
so small—like the food, Captain Motlow would say—but
I can't help that. It's the way I remember it.

Besides, it wasn't so small, after all.

We had lost all the rest of the night sealing up the holes
the arrows had made, and damned near didn't make ren-
dezvous at all; but Roche didn't seem to worry about that.
When we had finally been flamed and destroyed clean
enough to satisfy him, and Lea and I were let into the
control cabin of the *Chisholm*, he barely groused at us at
all. He was watching the films—not for the first time even
this soon, I could see—and he looked sick. Captain Motlow
was transparently puzzled, and also annoyed. Both of
them were too busy to speak to us, which made me furious,

and made Lea look more and more like the front side of the Mountains of Mitchell on Mars before the cap thaws.

"There is something about this situation that's all wrong," Dr. Roche said at last, mostly to himself. "And yet I can't quite put my finger on it."

"Everything was on schedule," Lea said shortly. I gathered that he felt he was being criticized.

"Yes, yes, it's not that. They responded to the stimuli exactly as you'd expect people in this kind of a culture to do. The games equations fall only when you haven't enough data about the enemy to fill in the parameters."

Sergeant Lea wore the expression of a Marine who suspects, quite rightly, that his own role in the action was being dismissed as also just part of the equations. Roche didn't notice.

"No, this isn't a question of behaviour. At least, I don't think it is. The trouble is, I don't know what it *is* a question of." He turned away from the screen as Bixby came in. "Ah. You were watching the action. Did you notice anything—peculiar? Would you like to see the films?"

"No," Doc Bixby said. He too was wearing a very odd expression. "I know what you're talking about, and I know the answer too. I've just been examining the patients. They're conscious and in good shape, so whenever you're ready to talk to them——"

"I'm ready now," Roche said, getting up. "But I'd better know what it is I'm missing. Please explain."

"It's a question of evolution," Doc Bixby said. "By what possible course of selection and mutation can a four-limbed vertebrate occupy the same planet as a six-legged one?"

Roche was stunned. He drew a long, slow breath.

"That's it," he said finally. "That's what threw me. I was looking at it, but I wasn't seeing it. The long torsos! They've got vestigial middle limbs folded under their clothing! Is that it?"

"Yes," Doc Bixby said. "Only they aren't vestigial. They're functional."

"Interesting. Well, I'm glad that's cleared up—I was afraid it was going to turn out to be something that made a difference."

"It *does*," Doc Bixby said. His expression was still very strange. Roche shot him a quick glance and hurried out towards the recovery room. Lea and the surgeon followed.

I stayed where I was for a while. I had to set up a departure orbit sooner or later, and it might as well be now. It would keep me occupied during the dry period of the interviewing, while Roche was perfecting his command of the language. Current heuristics can get a man through a language in about eight hours, but it's a deadly technical process, an ordeal to the student and absolutely unendurable to the bystander.

Captain Motlow watched my admittedly unusual display of forehandedness with considerable suspicion, but for once I didn't care. Doc Bixby's discovery may have resolved what had been bothering Dr. Roche—though from Bixby's expression it looked like Roche was due another discombobulation sooner or later—but it hadn't gotten past what was bothering me. That was the CONESTOGA business, of course.

As I have mentioned, the name came about by an accident unrelated to the Savannah affair. Ship's boats ordinarily aren't named at all, unless they bear the name of the parent ship. But when the *Chisholm* was on her shakedown cruise, some junior officer had made a joke about "hitting the Chisholm Trail"; and somebody else had remembered that the Conestoga wagon had been a machine with large, broad-rimmed wheels which had been specifically designed to ride well over soft soil.

And that's what a ship's gig is: a vessel designed to ride well in an atmosphere, not in a hard vacuum. It's essentially an airplane, not a spaceship. So they named the gig CONE-

STOGA; and after a while they got tired of it, as anyone tires of a joke that comes up again every time you look at a commonplace object, and forgot about it. But here it was back again.

Why did this bother me? I couldn't say. Partly, I suppose, because the *Chisholm* herself wasn't named after the Chisholm Trail, but after the first director of the World Medical Association, and perhaps the greatest. But that wasn't all; there was something else. And like Dr. Roche, I couldn't put my finger on it.

And even if I could, there would be nothing I could do about it. I was only an astrogator—and even if I had been Dr. Roche, the thing I was bothered about was too far in the past to be corrected, even by the theory of games.

So I thought; but like most people, I underestimated the viability of the past, the one thing the poets have been trying to pound into our corporate pinheads since words were invented:

> *We learn from words, but never learn much more*
> *than that from time to time the same things happen.*

But I wasn't then thinking about *The Folded and the Quiet*; the quotation didn't become attached to the Savannah affair in my mind until long afterward, when I encountered the poem during one of my dead-space reading jags. Now, I didn't really know what was the matter, and so all I could do was to continue to set up the tab board.

I missed the chow whistle too. Captain Motlow had to send up an orderly to fetch me.

Dr. Roche's patience was phenomenal, especially when you remembered the pressure of urgency under which he was labouring. Once he was able to talk to his eight charges with some facility, he did try at once to explain the situation to them. But it turned out that they were not in any mood to listen.

Nor could I blame them. After all, they were in the tank, which, provided though it was with every need Roche had been able to anticipate, was still utterly unlike any environment they had ever imagined, let alone encountered. As for Dr. Roche himself, he was to them a grossly magnified face on a wall—a face like those of the demons who had brought the plague in the first place, but huge and with a huge, disembodied voice to go with it. Roche was careful not to let any of the rest of us—the subsidiary demons—go drifting across the background of the screen, but it seemed to be too late for such precautions. The savages had already decided that they had been taken into the Underworld. They stood silently with their visible pairs of arms folded across their narrow chests, looking with sullen dignity into the face of the archdemon, waiting for judgment. They would not respond to any question except by giving their names, in a rapid rattle which went right around the circle, always in the same direction:

"Ukimfaa, Mwenzio, Kwa, Jua, Naye, Atakufaa, Kwa, Mvua."

Dr. Roche spoke briefly, was greeted by more silence, and turned the screen off, mopping his brow. "A stubborn lot," he said. "I expected it, but—I can't seem to get through it."

"Two of them have the same names," Doc Bixby noted.

"Yes, sir. They're all related—a clan, which is also a squad. 'Kwa' means 'if-then'; signifies that they're bound to each other, by blood and duty. That's the trouble."

"Do all the other names mean something too?" I asked.

"Yes, of course. Standard for this kind of society. The total makes up the squad, the functional fighting unit. But I don't have nearly enough data to work out the meanings of the connections. If I did, I could figure out which one of them is senior to the others, and concentrate on him. As it is, all I'm sure of is that neither Kwa can be; that's obviously a cousin-cousin crossover."

I almost didn't ask the next question. After all, I didn't know the language, and Dr. Roche did. But since he was obviously stumped, I couldn't see what harm it would do to introduce a little noise into the situation.

"Could it be grammatical? The connection, I mean?"

"What? Certainly not. No culture of this . . . Uh. Wait a minute. Why did you ask that, Hans?"

"Well, because they always name themselves in the same order. I thought just maybe, if the names all mean something, it might make up a sentence."

Roche bit his lip gently. After a few seconds, he said: "That's true, dammit. It does. It's condensed, though. Wait a minute."

He pulled a pad to him and wrote, very slowly and with the utmost effort, and then stared at what he had written.

"It says: RAINY SEASON/SOMEONE/HELP/HIM/ IF-THEN/DRY SEASON/MAYBE/YOU. By God, it's ____"

"The Golden Rule," Doc Bixby said softly. "Games theory; non-zero-sum theorem one."

"More than that. No, not more than that, but more useful to us right now. All these words are related, you see. You can't show that in English, but Savannahan is a highly inflected language; each of these eight words stands in a precise hierarchical relationship to all the other seven. The only grammatically unique word is 'help'; the others are duplicates, either in meaning or in function."

He took a deep breath and snapped the screen back on. "MWENZIO!" he shouted into the tank.

One of the tall tubular torsos stood abruptly as straight as a ramrod and came forward, the bullet head exalted.

"Mpo-kuseya," the savage cried, and waited.

"What's that mean?" Bixby whispered, offstage. It was a gross violation of Roche's rules, but Roche himself could not resist whispering back.

"It means: *I cannot fail.*"

88

The savage and the U.N.R.R.A. man stared at each other, as intently as though they were face to face, instead of watching images of each other. Then Roche began to speak once more, and now his urgency showed through at last.

I doubt that I could have followed him and Mwenzio even if I'd known the language; but I know now how it went, from the transcripts:

"Warrior, I charge you hear me, for the love of your children who may be kings. We have not come into the world to condemn. We have come to help."

"That is my name, demon."

"Then I bind you by it, for your children's sake."

"I am conquered," Mwenzio said. "Sorcery is sorcery; I bow the head. But my children are not yours to command, nor ever shall be."

"I promise you, in the name of your name, that I seek no such thing. It is the ill that I brought before that I come here to undo. To this I bind myself by my own name."

Both Captain Motlow and Doc Bixby stiffened at Roche's assumption of blame for what the first expedition had done, but Roche sensed it at once and drove them back with a slashing gesture, just below the level of the screen. Mwenzio said:

"What may I call you?"

"Mbote." ["Life."]

"Lokuta te?" ["This is no lie?"]

"Lokuta te, Mwenzio."

There was a long silence. Mwenzio stood still, with head bowed. Finally he said:

"Notice me, Mbote, your servant."

"Then it is this. I have told you of the plague and what needs to be done to combat it. Credit me now, for the time is very short. We will release you and all your clan, and you must carry the word to all the tribes and kingdoms.

You must persuade your kings and chieftains that those who brought the plague have come back with the cure, but only if all do exactly as we say it must be done. Above all, it must start at once, before the children are born. It would be best if all the mothers in the area where we put you down, all that can reach it by hard riding, should come to us."

"As we have done," Mwenzio said. "But then it is already too late."

"No, it can't be. Not for everyone. If we make haste——"

"No one can make haste backwards," Mwenzio said, and with a quick motion the short arms crossed above the bullet head, pulled the rough shirt up and off, and threw it to the floor of the tank. Without any visible signal, the other seven warriors shucked their shirts too, at the same moment.

In the cradle of each middle pair of arms, held low and flat across each narrow ventrum, six to eight Savannahan cubs squirmed over each other in a blind, brainless fury of nursing. They were about the size of chipmunks.

"We are the mothers," the warrior said. "And here are our children. They are already born. If it is not too late, then we give them to you, Mbote; cure them."

Nobody can know everything. The data about the Savannahans which the remains of the first expedition had brought back were reasonably complete—good enough to let Dr. Roche fill the parameters of his equations almost completely. But only *almost*. The first expedition hadn't been on Savannah long enough before the explosion to find out that the savages were six-limbed, let alone that the women were the warrior caste. As for us, we were culpable too— Doc Bixby most of all, for he had known the essential biological facts before Roche did, and had been keeping them to himself for the simple stupid pleasure of seeing Roche's face turn grey when the truth came out. I had felt that impulse myself now and then on Savannah, as I've already confessed, but I never did understand why the surgeon let it drive him—and all of us—so close to the rim of disaster. Roche only irritated me by being so knowing; but Bixby must really have hated him.

Bixby isn't with us any more, so I can't ask questions. Luckily for him, he had a great deal more up his sleeve than a simple surprise; otherwise he might have lost his licence, as well as been transferred, when the *Chisholm* got home. He took only a moment or so to savour Dr. Roche's shock and despair, and then said, loud enough for the savages to hear him (though not to understand him, because he said it in English):

"It's all right. The cubs are born as far as the savages are concerned, but medically they won't be born for another month yet."

"What do you mean?" Roche said. "Dammit, Clyde, you'll pay for this. If you'd spoken earlier——"

"I spoke soon enough," Doc Bixby said, but he retreated a little from the savagery in Roche's voice. "The cubs are embryologically immature, that's all. From the point of view of development, they're still foetuses. They seem to get born as soon as they can control their muscles, and then they crawl up into the dam's arms to be nursed the rest of the way to 'term'—like marsupials on Earth. I knew it would be that way as soon as I realized that these creatures had to have two functional pelvic girdles. If those bones are to be in balance well enough to serve as fulcrums for *two* pairs of hind limbs—and you can see that that's what the original situation was by looking at the 'horses'—then neither of them could simultaneously be flexible enough to pass a full-term cub. It was much more likely that they littered very early and maintained the whelps *outside* the womb until they reached term. They probably have many more children than they ever manage to raise; the weak ones just don't manage to make it into the nursing arms, and fall off to die. A good system for selecting out weak sisters—

brutal for the spawn, but kind to the race. That's evolution for you every time."

"Very like the marsupials," Roche said in a flat, quiet voice.

"Yes, just as I said."

"What did evolution ever do for the marsupials? Opossums and kangaroos are notably inefficient animals. They've shucked off their weak sisters that way for millions of years, and still they're no better equipped to survive than they ever were! But never mind, we can't change that. What I want to know is, can we still immunize these cubs? Are they still unborn in *that* sense? In short, Clyde, now that your practical joke is over—*is there still time*? I've made promises. Can I keep them?"

"I didn't . . . Sure you can. I took blood samples and ran antibody titers on one of the cubs when I first discovered this. They're naturally immune until they're 'born'; they're getting the appropriate beta-globulins from their mothers' milk. You can save them."

"No thanks to you," Roche said in a raw, ragged whisper.

"No," Bixby said. Abruptly, he looked quite haggard. "I suppose not. All I can say is, I would have spoken before you promised anything if it had really been too late. But there is still time."

In the tank, the warriors held out their children.

It went very well after that, all things considered. By the time we left, the plague was greatly slowed down, and Roche and the computer between them were convinced that it would cease to be an important pandemic on Savannah not long after the *Chisholm* left. It wouldn't be exterminated, of course. Now that it had been established in so many living cells, the virus would be passed on, from generation to generation, protected in its intracellular environment from any possible concentration of antibodies circulating in the extracellular fluids of the body. But by that same token, this chronic infection would keep the antibody titers high, and prevent the virus from causing any overt illness. The immunity would stick, which was what we had sought, and what we brought about.

It was over.

Except that I have come up at last with what it was that had been bothering me the whole time. And it was not just a fantasm, not just a crotchet. It was real, and came crawling into my head in all its unavoidable dread and revulsion at the moment that I opened my new orders, and found that I was again assigned to be the astrogator of the *Chisholm*.

At that instant, I remembered that the Conestoga wagon was the machine that brought tuberculosis to the Indians . . . and the orders say that we are on our way back to Savannah.

A Dusk of Idols

Nietzsche's book of the same title was of course the main
source of this story, which won one of Judith Merril's
round one hundred Honourable Mentions for its year, but
the approach—as several readers noticed—is out of
Conrad, with Marlowe thrown in for misdirection. Since
there's no money to be divided up, presumably they get
the Honour and I get the Mention.

I can tell you now what happened to Naysmith. He hit
Chandala.

Quite by coincidence—he was on his way home at the
time—but it caught him. It was in all respects a most
peculiar accident. The chances were against it, including
that I should have heard anything about it.

Almost everyone in Arm II knows that Chandala is, pre-
eminently among civilized planets, a world in mortal agony
—and a world about which, essentially, nothing can be done.
Naysmith didn't know it. He had had no experience of
Arm II and was returning along it from his first contact
with the Heart stars when his ship (and mine) touched
Chandala briefly. He was on his way back to Earth (which
technically is an Arm II planet, but so far out in the hinter-
lands that no Earthman ever thinks of it as such) when this
happened, and since it happened during ship's night, he
would never have known the difference if it hadn't been for an
attack of simple indigestion which awakened him—and me.

It's very hard to explain the loss of so eminent a surgeon
as Naysmith without maligning his character, but as his

only confidant, more or less, I don't seem to have much of a choice. The fact is that he should have been the last person in the Galaxy to care about Chandala's agony. He had used his gifts to become exclusively a rich man's surgeon; as far as I know, he had never done any time in a clinic after his residency days. He had gone to the Heart stars only to sterilize, for a very large fortune in fees, the sibling of the Bbiben of Bbenaf—for the fees, and for the additional fortune the honour would bring him later. Bbenaf law requires that the operation be performed by an off-worlder, but Naysmith was the first Earthman to be invited to do it.

But if during the trip there or back some fellow passenger had come down with a simple appendicitis, Naysmith wouldn't have touched him. He would have said, with remote impartiality, that that was the job of the ship's surgeon (me). If for some reason I had been too late to help, Naysmith still would not have lifted a finger.

There are not supposed to be any doctors like that, but there are. Nobody should assume that I think they are in the majority—they are in fact very rare—but I see no point in pretending that they don't exist. They do; and the eminent Naysmith was one of them. He was in fact almost the Platonic ideal of such a doctor. And you do not have to be in the Heart stars to begin to think of the Hippocratic Oath as being quaint, ancient, and remote. You can become isolated from it just as easily on Earth, by the interposition of unclimbable mountains of money, if you share Naysmith's temperament.

His temperament, to put it very simply, was that of a pathologically depressed man carrying a terrible load of anxiety. In him, it showed up by making him a hypochondriac, and I don't think he would ever have gone into medicine at all had it not been for an urgent concern about his own health which set in while he was still in college.

I had known him slightly then, and was repelled by him. He was always thinking about his own innards. Nothing pleased him, nothing took him out of himself, he had no eye for any of the elegance and the beauty of the universe outside his own skin. Though he was as brilliant a man as I ever knew, he was a bore, the kind of bore who replies to "How are you?" by telling you how he is, in clinical detail. He was forever certain that his liver or his stomach or some other major organ had just quit on him and was going to have to be removed—probably too suddenly for help to be summoned in time.

It seems inarguable to me, though I am not a psychologist, that he took up medicine primarily in the hope (unrecognized in his own mind) of being able to assess his own troubles better, and treat them himself when he couldn't get another doctor to take them as seriously as he did. Of course this did not work. It is an old proverb in medicine that the man who treats himself has a fool for a physician, which is only a crude way of saying that the doctor-patient relationship absolutely requires that there be two people involved. A man can no more be his own doctor than he can be his own wife, no matter how much he knows about marriage or medicine.

The result was that even after becoming the kind of surgeon who gets called across 50,000 light-years to operate on the sibling of the Bbiben of Bbenaf, he was still a hypochondriac. In fact, he was worse off than ever, because he now had the most elaborate and sophisticated knowledge of all the obscure things that might be wrong with him. He had a lifelong case of interne's syndrome, the cast of mind which makes beginners in medicine sure that they are suffering from everything they have just read about in the textbook. He knew this; he was, as I have said, a brilliant man; though he had reached his ostensible goal, he was now in a position where he did not *dare* to treat himself, even for the hiccups.

And this was why he called me at midnight, ship's time, to look him over. There was nothing curable the matter with him. He had eaten something on Bbenaf—though he was a big, burly, bearded man, immoderate eating had made him unpleasantly soft—that was having trouble accommodating itself to his Terrestrial protein complement. I judged that tomorrow he would have a slight rash, and thereafter the episode would be over. I told him so.

"Um. Yes. Daresay you're right. Still rather a shock though, to be brought bolt upright like that in the middle of the night."

"Of course. However, I'm sure it's nothing more than a slight food allergy—the commonest of all tourist complaints," I added, a little maliciously. "The tablets are antihistaminic, of course. They ought to head off any serious sequelae, and make you a little sleepy to boot. You could use the relaxation, I think."

He nodded absently, without taking any apparent notice of my mean little dig. He did not recognize me, I was quite sure. It had been a long time since college.

"Where are we?" he said. He was wide awake, though his alarm reaction seemed to be wearing off, and he didn't seem to want to take my hint that he use the pills as sleepy drugs; he wanted company, at least for a little while. Well, I was curious, too. He was an eminent man in my own profession, and I had an advantage over him: I knew more about him than he thought I did. If he wanted to talk, I was delighted to let him.

"Chandala, I believe. A real running sore of a planet, but we won't be here long; it's just a message stop."

"Oh? What's the matter with the place? Barbaric?"

"No, not in the usual sense. It's classified as a civilized planet. It's just sick, that's all. Most of the population is being killed off."

"A pandemic?" Naysmith said slowly. "That doesn't sound like a civilized planet."

97

"It's hard to explain," I said. "It's not just one plague. There are scores of them going. I suppose the simple way to put it is to say that the culture of Chandala doesn't believe in sanitation—but that's not really true either. They believe in it, thoroughly, but they don't practise it very much. In fact a large part of the time they practise it in reverse."

"In reverse? That doesn't make any sense."

"I warned you it was hard to explain. I mean that public health there is a privilege. The ruling classes make it unavailable to the people they govern, as a means of keeping them in line."

"But that's insane!" Naysmith exclaimed.

"I suppose it is, by our ideas. It's obviously very hard to keep under control, anyhow; the rulers often suffer as much as the ruled. But all governments are based on the monopoly of the right to use violence—only the weapons vary from planet to planet. This one is Chandala's. And the Heart stars have decided not to interfere."

He fell silent. I probably had not needed to remind him that what the federation we call the Heart stars decided to do, or not to do, was often very difficult to riddle. Its records reach back about a million years, which, however, cover only its period of stability. Probably it is as much as twice that old. No Arm II planet belonged to the group yet. Earth could be expected to be allowed to join in about forty-five thousand years—and that was what remained of half our originally allotted trial period; the cut was awarded us after our treaty with the star-dwelling race of Angels. In the meantime, we could expect no help . . . nor could Chandala. Earth was fortunate to be allowed any intercourse whatsoever with the Heart stars; there again, we could thank the Angels—who live forever—for vouching for us.

"Dr. Rosenbaum," Naysmith said slowly, "do you think that's right and proper?"

So he had recognized me after all. He would never have bothered to look up my name on the roster.

"Well, no, I suppose not. But the rule is that every planet is to be allowed to go to hell in its own handbasket. It isn't my rule, or the Earth's rule; but there it is. The Heart stars just won't be bothered with any world that can't achieve stability by itself. They have seen too many of them come and go."

"I think there's more to it than that. Some of the planets that failed to get into the federation failed because they got into planetwide wars—or into wars with each other."

"Sure," I said, puzzled. "That's just the kind of thing the Heart stars have no use for."

"So they didn't interfere to stop the wars."

"No." Now I was beginning to see what he was driving at, but he bore down on me relentlessly all the same.

"So there is in fact no Heart-star rule that we can't help Chandala if we want to. In fact, doing so may not even prejudice our case with the federation. We just don't know."

"I suppose that's true, but——"

"And, in fact, it might help us? We don't know that either?"

"No, we don't," I admitted, but my patience was beginning to run out. It had been a long night. "All we do know is that the Heart stars follow certain rules of their own. Common sense suggests that our chances would be best if we followed them, too."

"Common sense for our remotely imaginable great-great-greatest of grandchildren, maybe. But by then conditions will have changed beyond our remotest imaginings. Half a millennium!"

"They don't change in the Heart stars. That's the whole point—stability. And above all, I'd avoid picking up a stick of TDX like Chandala. It's obviously just the kind of non-survival planet the Heart stars *mean* to exclude by their rules. There'd be nothing you could do with it but blow yourself up. And there's obviously nothing we could do *for* it, anyhow!"

"Gently now, Doctor. Are you sure of that? Sanitation isn't the only public-health technique there is."

"I don't follow you," I said. The fact is that by now I wasn't trying very hard.

"Well," Naysmith said, "consider that there was once a thing called the Roman Empire. It owned all the known world and lasted many centuries. But fifty men with modern weapons could have conquered it, even when it was at its most powerful."

"But the Heart stars——"

"I am not talking about the Heart stars. I'm talking about Chandala. Two physicians with modern field kits could have wiped out almost all the diseases that raddled the Roman Empire. For instance, you and I."

I swallowed and looked at my watch. We were still a good two hours away from takeoff time.

"No, Doctor, you'll have to answer me. Shall we try it?"

I could still stall, though I was not hopeful that it would help me much. "I don't understand your motives, Dr. Naysmith. What do you want to try it *for*? The Chandalese are satisfied with their system. They won't thank you for trying to upset it. And where's the profit? I can't see any."

"What kind of profit are you talking about?" Naysmith said, almost abstractedly.

"Well . . . I don't know; that's what I'm asking you. It seems to me you shouldn't lack for money by now. And as for honour, you're up to your eyebrows in that already, and after Bbenaf you'll have much more. And yet you seem to be proposing to throw all that away for a moribund world you never heard of until tonight. And your life, too. They would kill you instantly down there if they knew what you had in mind."

"I don't plan to tell the ruling class, whatever that is, what I have in mind," Naysmith said. "I have that much sense.

As for my motives . . . they're properly my own. But I can satisfy your curiosity a little. I know what you see when you look at me: a society doctor. It's not an unusual opinion. My record supports it. Isn't that true?"

I didn't nod, but my silence must have given my assent.

"Yes, it's true, of course. And if I had excuses, I wouldn't give a damn for your opinion—or for Chandala. But you see, I don't. I not only know what the opinion of me is, but *I share it myself*. Now I see a chance to change that opinion of me; not yours, but mine. Does that help you any?"

It did. Every man has his own Holy Grail. Naysmith had just identified his.

"I wish you luck."

"But you won't go along?"—

"No," I said, miserable, yet defiantly sure that there were *no* good reasons why I should join Naysmith's quest—not even the reason that it could not succeed without me and my field kit. It could not succeed *with* me, either; and my duty lay with the ship, until the day when I might sight my own Grail, whatever that might be. All the same, that one word made me feel like an assassin.

But it did not surprise Naysmith. He had had the good sense to expect nothing else. Whatever the practical notions that had sprung into his head in the last hour or so, and I suppose they were many, he must have known all his life—as we all do—that Grail-hunting is essentially the loneliest of hobbies.

He made himself wholly unpopular on the bridge, which up to now had barely known he was aboard, wangling a ship's gig and a twenty-four-hour delay during which he could be force-fed the language of the nearest city-state by a heuristics expert, and then disembarked. The arrangement was that we were to pick him up on our next cruise, a year from now.

If he had to get off the planet before then, he could go

into orbit and wait; he had supplies enough. He also had his full field medical kit, including a space suit. Since it is of the nature of Chandalese political geography to shift without notice, he agreed to base himself on the edge of a volcanic region which we could easily identify from space, yet small enough so that we wouldn't have to map it to find the gig.

Then he left. Everything went without incident (he told me later) until he entered the city-state of Gandu, whose language he had and where our embassy was. He had of course been told that the Chandalese, though humanoid, are three times as tall as Earthmen, but it was a little unnerving all the same to walk among them. Their size suited their world, which was a good twelve thousand miles in diameter. Surprisingly, it was not very dense, a fact nobody had been able to explain, since it was obviously an Earthlike planet; hence there was no gravitational impediment to growing its natives very large, and grow large they did. He would have to do much of his doctoring here on a stepladder, apparently.

The chargé d'affaires at the embassy, like those of us on ship, did his best to dissuade Naysmith.

"I don't say that you can't do something about the situation here," he said. "Very likely you can. But you'll be meddling with their social structure. Public health here is politics, and vice versa. The Heart stars——"

"Bother the Heart stars," Naysmith said, thereby giving the chargé d'affaires the worst fright he had had in years. "If it can be done, it ought to be done. And the best way to do it is to go right to the worst trouble spot."

"That would be Iridu, down the river some fifteen miles," the chargé d'affaires said. "Dying out very rapidly. But it's proscribed, as all those places are."

"Criminal. What about language?"

"Oh, same as here. It's one of three cities that spoke the same tongue. The third one is dead."

"Where do I go to see the head man?"

"To the sewer. He'll be there."

Naysmith stared.

"Well, I'm sorry, but that's the way things are. When you came through the main plaza here, did you see two tall totem poles?"

"Yes."

"The city totems always mark the local entrance to the Grand Sewer of Chandala, and the big stone building behind them is always where the priest-chief lives. And I'm warning you, Dr. Naysmith, he won't give you the time of day."

Naysmith did not bother to argue any more. It seemed to him that no matter how thoroughly a chieftain may subscribe to a political system, he becomes a rebel when it is turned against him—especially if as a consequence he sees his people dying all around him. He left, and went downriver, on a vessel rather like a felucca.

He had enough acumen to realize very early that he was being trailed. One of the two Chandalese following him looked very like a man who had been on duty at the embassy. He did not let it bother him, and in any event, they did not seem to follow him past the gates of Iridu.

He found the central plaza easily enough—that is to say, he was never lost; the physical act of getting through the streets was anything but easy, though he was towing his gear on an antigrav unit. They were heaped with refuse and bodies. Those who still lived made no attempt to clear away the dead or help the dying, but simply sat in the doorways and moaned. The composite sound thrummed through the whole city. Now and then he saw small groups scavenging for food amid all the garbage; and quite frequently he saw individuals drinking from puddles. This last fact perplexed him particularly, for the chargé d'affaires had told him plainly that Chandala boasted excellent water-supply systems.

The reception of the priest-chief was hostile enough, more so than Naysmith had hoped, yet less than the chargé d'affaires had predicted—at least at first. He was obviously sick himself, and seemingly had not bathed in a long time, nor had any of his attendants; but as long as all Naysmith wanted was information, he was grudgingly willing to give it.

"What you observe are the Articles of the Law and their consequences," he said. "Because of high failures before the gods, Iridu and all its people have been abased to the lowest caste; and since it is not meet that people of this caste speak the same tongue as the Exalted, the city is proscribed."

"I can understand that," Naysmith said, guardedly. "But why should that prevent you from taking any care of yourselves? Drinking from puddles——"

"These are the rules for our caste," the priest-chief said. "Not to wash; not to eat aught less than three days old; not to aid the sick or bury the dead. Drinking from puddles is graciously allowed us."

There was no apparent ironic intention in the last sentence. Naysmith said, "Graciously?"

"The water in the city's plumbing now comes directly from the Grand Sewer. The only other alternative is the urine of the anah, but that is for holy men doing penance for the people."

This was a setback. Without decent water he would be sadly handicapped, and obviously what came out of the faucets was not under the control of the doomed city.

"Well, we'll manage somehow. Rain barrels should serve for the time being; I can chlorinate them for you. But it's urgent to start cleaning things up; otherwise, I'll never be able to keep up with all the new cases. Will you help me?"

The priest-chief looked blank. "We can help no one any more, little one."

"You could be a big help. I can probably stop this plague for you, with a few willing hands."

104

The priest-chief stood up, shakily, but part of his shakiness was black rage. "To break the rules of caste is the highest of failures before the gods," he said. "We are damned to listen to such counsels! Kill him!"

Naysmith was fool enough to pause to protest. Only the fact that most of the gigantic soldiers in the chamber were clumsy with disease, and unused to dealing with so small an object as he, got him out of the building alive. He was pursued to the farther gate of Iridu by a shambling and horrible mob, all the more frightening because there was hardly a healthy creature in its ranks.

Outside, he was confronted by a seemingly trackless jungle. He plunged in at hazard, and kept going blindly until he could no longer hear the noise of the pack; evidently they had stopped at the gate. He could thank the proscription of the city-nation for that.

On the other hand, he was lost.

Of course, he had his compass, which might help a little. He did not want to go westward, which would take him back to the river, but also into the vicinity of Iridu again. Besides, his two trackers from Gandu might still be lurking at the west gate, and this time their hostility might be a good deal more active. Striking north-northwest towards Gandu itself was open to the same objection. There seemed to be nothing for it but to go north-northeast, in the hope of arriving at the field of fumaroles and hot springs where his ship was, there to take thought.

He was still utterly determined to try again; shaken though he was, he was convinced that this first failure was only a matter of tactics. But he did have to get back to the ship.

He pushed forward through the wiry tangle. It made it impossible for him to follow a straight compass course; he lost hours climbing and skirting and hacking, and began to worry about the possibility of spending the night in this wilderness. With the thought, there was a sodden thump behind him, and he was stopped as though he had run into a wall. Then there was a diminishing crackle and bumping over his head.

What was holding him back, he realized after a moment, was the tow to his gear. He backtracked. The gear was lying on the moist ground. Some incredibly tough vine had cut the antigrav unit free of it; the other sound he heard had been the unit fighting its way skyward.

Now what? He could not possibly drag all this weight. It occurred to him that he might put on the space suit; that would slow him a good deal, but it would also protect him from the underbrush, which had already slashed him pretty painfully. The rest of the load—a pack and two oxygen bottles—would still be heavy, but maybe not impossibly so.

He got the suit on, though it was difficult without help, and lumbered forward again. It was exhausting, even with the suit's air conditioning to help, but there was nothing he could do about that. At least, if he had to sleep in the jungle, the suit might also keep out vermin, and some larger entities. . . .

For some reason, however, the Chandalese forest seemed peculiarly free of large animals. Occasional scamperings and brief glimpses told of creatures which might have been a little like antelope, or like rabbits, but even these were scarce; and there were no cries of predators. This might have been because Chandalese predators were voiceless, but Naysmith doubted this on grounds of simple biology; it seemed more likely that most of the more highly organized wildlife of Chandala had long since been decimated by the plagues the owners of the planet cultivated as though they were ornamental gardens.

Late in the afternoon, the fates awarded him two lucky breaks. The first of these was a carcass, or rather, a shell. It was the greenish-brown carapace of some creature which, from its size, he first took to be the Chandalese equivalent of a huge land turtle, but on closer examination seemed actually to have been a good deal more like a tick. Well, if any planet had ticks as big as rowboats, it would be Chandala, that much was already plain even to Naysmith. In any event, the shell made an excellent skid for his gear, riding on its back through the undergrowth almost as though it had been designed for the task.

The second boon was the road. He did not recognize it as such at first, for it was much broken and overgrown, but on reflection he decided that this was all to the good; a road that had not been in use for a long time would be a road on which he would be unlikely to meet anybody. It would also not be likely to take him to any populated place, but it seemed to be headed more or less in the direction he wanted to go; and if it meandered a little, it could hardly impose upon him more detours than the jungle did.

He took off the space suit and loaded it into the skid, feeling almost cheerful.

It was dusk when he rounded the bend and saw the dead city. In the gathering gloom, it looked to be almost twice the size of Gandu, despite the fact that much of it had crumbled and fallen.

At its open gates stood the two Chandalese who had followed him downriver, leaning on broad-bladed spears as tall as they were.

Naysmith had a gun, and he did not hesitate.

Had he not recognized the face of the Chandalese from the chargé d'affaires' office, he might have assumed that the two guards were members of some savage tribe. Again, it seemed to him, he had been lucky.

It might be the last such stroke of luck. The presence of the guards testified, almost in letters of fire, that the Chandalese could predict his route with good accuracy—and the spears testified that they did not mean to let him complete it.

Again, it seemed to him that his best chance led through the dead city, protected while he was there by its proscription. He could only hope that the firelands lay within some reachable distance of the city's other side.

The ancient gate towered over him like the Lion Gate of Mycenae as remembered from some nightmare—fully as frowning as that narrow, heavy, tragedy-ridden breach, but more than five times as high. He studied it with sober respect, and perhaps even a little dread, before he could bring himself to step over the bodies of the guards and pass through it. When he did, he was carrying with him one of the broad-bladed fifteen-foot spears, because, he told himself, you never could tell when such a lever might come in handy . . . and because, instinctively, he believed (though he later denied it) that no stranger could pass under that ancient arch without one.

The Atridae, it is very clear, still mutter in their sleep not far below the surface of our waking minds, for all that we no longer allow old Freud to cram our lives back into the straitjackets of those old religious plays. Perhaps one of the changes in us that the Heart stars await is the extirpation of these last shadows of Oedipus, Elektra, Agamemnon, and all those other dark and bloody figures, from the way we think.

Or maybe not. There are still some forty thousand years to go. If after that they tell us that that was one of the things they were waiting for, we probably won't understand what they're talking about.

Carrying the spear awkwardly and towing his belongings behind him in the tick shell, Naysmith plodded towards the centre of the dead city. There was nothing left in the streets but an occasional large bone; one that he stumbled over fell promptly to slivers and dust. The scraping noise of his awkward sledge echoed off the fronts of the leaning buildings; otherwise, there was no sound but the end-stopped thuds of his footfalls, and an occasional bluster of evening wind around the tottering, flaking cornices far above his bent head.

In this wise he came draggingly at last into the central plaza, and sat down on a drum of a fallen stone pillar to catch his breath. It was now almost full dark, so dark that nothing cast a shadow any more; instead, the night seemed to be soaking into the ground all around him. There would be, he knew already, no stars; the atmosphere of Chandala was too misty for that. He had perhaps fifteen minutes more to decide what he was going to do.

As he mopped his brow and tried to think, something rustled behind him. Freezing, he looked carefully over his shoulder, back towards the way he had come. Of course he saw nothing; but in this dead silence a sound like that was easy to interpret.

They were still following him. For him, this dead city was not a proscripted sanctuary. Or if it ever had been, it was no longer, since he had killed the two guards.

He stood up, as soundlessly as he could. All his muscles were aching; he felt as soft and helpless as an overripe melon. The shuffling noise stopped at once.

They were already close enough to see him!

He knew that he could vanish quickly enough into any of the tomblike buildings around him, and evade them for a while as deftly as any rat. They probably knew this labyrinth little better than he did, and the sound of their shuffling did not suggest that there were many of them—surely not a large enough force to search a whole city for a man only a third as big as a Chandalese. And they would have to respect taboos that he could scamper past out of simple ignorance.

But if he took that way, he would have to abandon his gear. He could carry his medical kit easily enough, but that was less important to him now than the space suit and its ancillary oxygen bottles—both heavy and clumsy, and both, furthermore, painted white. As long as he could drag them

109

with him in the tick shell, their whiteness would be masked to some extent; but if he had to run with them, he would surely be brought down.

In the last remains of the evening, he stood cautiously forward and inched the sledge towards the centre of the plaza, clenching the spear precariously against his side under one armpit, his gun in his other hand. Behind him, something went, *scuffle . . . rustle. . . .*

As he had seen on arrival, the broad-mouthed well in the centre of the plaza, before the house of the dead and damned priest-chief, was not flanked by the totems he had been taught to expect. Where they should be jutted only two grey and splintered stumps, as though the poles had been pushed over by brute force and toppled into the abyss. On the other side of the well, a stone beast—an anah?—stared forever downward with blind eyes, ready to rend any soul who might try to clamber up again from Hell.

As it might try to do; for a narrow, rail-less stone stairway, slimy and worn, spiralled around the well into the depths.

Around the mouth of the well, almost impossible to see, let alone interpret, in the last glimmers, was a series of bas-reliefs, crudely and hastily cut; he could detect the rawness of the sculpturing even under the weathering of the stone and the moss.

He went cautiously down the steps a little way to look at them. With no experience whatsoever of Chandalese graphic conventions, he knew that he had little chance of understanding them even had he seen them in full daylight. Nevertheless, it was clear that they told a history . . . and, it seemed to him, a judgment. This city had been condemned, and its totems toppled, because it had been carrying on some kind of congress with the Abyss.

He climbed back to the surface of the plaza, pulling his nose thoughtfully. They were still following him, that was sure. But would they follow him down there? It might be a way to get to the other side of the dead city which would promise him immunity—or at least, a temporary sanctuary of an inverted kind.

He did not delude himself that he could live down there for long. He would have to wear the space suit again, and breathe nothing but the oxygen in the white bottles. He could still keep by him the field medical kit with which he had been planning to re-enrich his opinion of himself, and save a planet; but even with this protection he could not for long breathe the air and drink the water of the pit. As for food, that hardly mattered, because his air and water would run out much sooner.

Let it be said that Naysmith was courageous. He donned the space suit again, and began the descent, lowering his tick-shell coracle before him on a short, taut tether. Bump, bump, bump went the shell down the steps ahead of him, teetering on its back ridge, threatening to slip sidewise and fall into the well at every irregularity in the slimy old platforms. Then he would stop in the blackness and wait until he could no longer hear it rocking. Then down again: bump, bump, bump; step, step, step. Behind him, the butt of the spear scraped against the wall; and once the point lodged abruptly in some chink and nearly threw him.

He had his chest torch going, but it was not much help; the slimy walls of the well seemed to soak up the light, except for an occasional delusive reflection where a rill of seepage oozed down amid the nitre. Down, down, down.

After some centuries, he no longer expected to reach the bottom. There was nothing left in his future but this painful descent. He was still not frightened; only numb, exhausted, beyond caring about himself, beyond believing in the rest of the universe.

Then the steps stopped, sending him staggering in the suit. He touched the wall with a glove—he imagined that he could feel its coldness, though of course he could not—and stood still. His belt radios brought him in nothing but a sort of generalized echo, like running water.

111

Of course. He flashed the chest light around, and saw the Grand Sewer of Chandala.

He was standing on what appeared to be a wharf made of black basalt, over the edge of which rushed the black waters of an oily river, topped with spinning masses of soapy froth. He could not see the other side, nor the roof of the tunnel it ran in—only the sullen and ceaseless flood, like a cataract of ink. The wharf itself had evidently been awash not long since, for there were still pools standing sullenly wherever the black rock had been worn down; but now the surface of the river was perhaps a foot below the level of the dock.

He looked up. Far aloft, he saw a spot of blue-black sky about the size of a pea, and gleaming in it, one reddish star. Though he was no better judge of distance than any other surgeon or any other man who spends his life doing close work, he thought he was at least a mile beneath the surface. To clamber back up there would be utterly beyond him.

But why a wharf? Who would be embarking on this sunless river, and why? It suggested that the river might go towards some other inhabited place . . . or some place that had once been inhabited. Maybe the Chandalese had been right in condemning the city to death for congress with the pit—and if that Other Place were inhabited even now, it was probably itself underground, and populated by whatever kind of thing might enjoy and prosper by living in total darkness by the side of a sewer—

There was an ear-splitting explosion to Naysmith's right, and something struck his suit just under his armpit. He jerked his light towards the sound, just in time to see fragments of rock scampering away across the wet wharf, skidding and splashing. A heavier piece rolled eccentrically to the edge of the dock and dropped off into the river. Then everything was motionless again.

He bent and picked up the nearest piece. It was part of one of the stones of the staircase.

There was no sanctuary, even here; they were following him down. In a few moments it might occur to them to stone him on purpose; the suit could stand that, but the helmet could not. And above all, he had to keep his air pure.

He had to go on. But there was no longer any walkway; only the wharf and the sewer. Well, then, that way. Grimly he unloaded the tick shell and lowered it into the black water, hitching its tether to a basalt post. Then, carefully, he ballasted it with the pack and the oxygen bottles. It rocked gently in the current, but the ridge along its back served as a rudimentary keel; it would be stable, more or less.

He sat down on the edge of the wharf and dangled his feet into his boat while he probed for the bottom of the river with the point of the spear. The point caught on something after he had thrust nearly twelve feet of the shaft beneath the surface; and steadying himself with this, he transferred his weight into the coracle and sat down.

Smash! Another paving stone broke on the dock. A splinter, evidently a large one, went whooshing past his helmet and dropped into the sewer. Hastily, he jerked the loop of the tether off the basalt post, and poled himself hard out into the middle of the torrent.

The wharf vanished. The shell began to turn round and round. After several minutes, during which he became nearly seasick, Naysmith managed to work out how to use the blade of the spear as a kind of steering oar; if he held it hard against one side of the shell at the back, and shifted the shaft with the vagaries of the current, he could at least keep his frail machine pointed forward.

There was no particular point in steering it any better than that, since he did not know where he was going.

The chest light showed him nothing except an occasional glimpse of a swiftly passing tunnel wall, and after a while he shut it off to conserve power, trusting his sense of balance to keep his shell headed forward and in the middle of the current. Then he struck some obstacle which almost upset him; and though he fought himself back into balance again, the shell seemed sluggish afterwards. He put on the light and discovered that he had shipped so much of the slimy water that the shell was riding only a few inches above the roiling river.

He ripped the flap of his pack open and found a cup to bail with. Thereafter, he kept the light on.

After a while, the noise of the water took on a sort of hissing edge. He hardly noticed it at first; but soon it became sharp, like the squeak of a wet finger on the edge of a glass, and then took on deeper tones until it made the waters boil like the noise of a steam whistle. Turning the belt radio down did him very little good; it dropped the volume of the sound, but not its penetrating quality.

Then the coracle went skidding around a long bend and light burst over him.

He was hurtling past a city, fronted by black basalt docks like the one he had just quitted, but four or five times more extensive. Beyond these were ruins, as far as he could see, tumbled and razed, stark in the unwavering flare of five tall, smokeless plumes of gas flames which towered amid the tumbled stones. It was these five fountains of blue-white fire, as tall as sequoias, which poured out the vast organ-diapason of noise he had heard in the tunnel.

They were probably natural, though he had never seen anything like them before. The ruins, much more obviously, were not; and for them there was no explanation. Broken and aged though they were, the great carved stones still preserved the shapes of geometrical solids which could not possibly have been reassembled into any building Naysmith could imagine, though as a master surgeon he had traded all his life on structural visualization. The size of the pieces did not bother him, for he had come to terms with the fact

114

that the Chandalese were three times as tall as men, but their shapes were as irrational as the solid geometry of a dream.

And the crazy way in which the city had been dumped over, as though something vast and stupid had sat down in the middle of it and lashed a long heavy tail, did not suggest that its destroyers had been Chandalese either.

Then it was gone. He clung to his oar, keeping the coracle pointed forward. He did not relish the thought of going on to a possible meeting with the creatures who had razed that city; but obviously there had been no hope for him in its ruins. It dwindled and dimmed, and then he went wobbling around a bend and even its glow vanished from the sides of the tunnel.

As he turned that corner, something behind him shrieked, cutting through the general roar of noise like a god in torture. He shrank down into the bottom of the boat, almost losing his hold on the spear. The awful yell must have gone on for two or three minutes, utterly overpowering every echo. Then, gradually, it began to die, at first into a sort of hopeless howl, then into a series of raw, hoarse wails, and at last into a choked mixture of weeping and giggling . . . oh! oooh! . . . whee! . . . oh, oh, oh . . . whee! . . . which made Naysmith's every hair stand on end. It was, obviously, only one of the high-pressure gas jets fluting over a rock lip.

Obviously.

After that he was glad to be back in the darkness, however little it promised. The boat bobbed and slithered in the midst of the flood. On turns it was washed against the walls and Naysmith poled it back into the centre of the current as best he could with his break-bone spear, which kept knocking him about the helmet and ribs every time he tried to use it for anything but steering. Some of those collisions were inexplicably soft; he did not try to see why, because he was saving the chest light for bailing, and in any event he was swept by them too fast to look back.

A Dusk of Idols

Just under him gurgled the Grand Sewer of Chandala, a torrent of filth and pestilence. He floated down it inside his suit, Naysmith, master surgeon, a bubble of precarious life in a universe of corruption, skimming the entropy gradient, clinging to the edges of a tick's carapace . . . and clinging to incorruption to the last.

Again, after a while, he saw light ahead, sullenly red at first, but becoming more and more orange as the boat swept on. For the first time he saw the limits of the tunnel, outlined ahead of him in the form of a broad arch. Could he possibly be approaching the surface? It did not seem possible; it was night up there—and besides, Chandalese daylight was nothing like this.

Then the tunnel mouth was behind him, and he was coasting on an enormous infernal sea.

The light was now a brilliant tangerine colour, but he could not see where it came from; billowing clouds of mist rising from the surface of the sewage limited visibility to perhaps fifty feet. The current from the river was quickly dissipated, and the coracle began to drift sidewise; probing with the spear without much hope, he was surprised to touch bottom, and began to pole himself forward with the aid of his compass—though he had almost forgotten why it was that he had wanted to go in that direction.

The bottom was mucky, as was, of course, to be expected; pulling the spear out of it was tiring work. Far overhead in the mists, he twice heard an odd fluttering sound, rather like that of a tightly wound rubber band suddenly released, and once a measured flapping which seemed to pass quite low over his head; he saw nothing, however.

After half an hour he stopped poling to give himself five minutes' rest. Again he began to drift sidewise. In so far as he could tell, the whole of this infernal deep seemed to be eddying in a slow circle.

Then a tall, slender shadow loomed ahead of him. He

116

drove the spear into the bottom and anchored himself, watching intently, but the shadow remained fixed. Finally he pushed the shell cautiously towards it.

It was a totem pole, obviously very old; almost all its paint was gone, and the exposed wood was grey. There were others ahead; within a few moments he was in what was almost a forest of them, their many mute faces grinning and grimacing at him or staring hopelessly off into the mists. Some of them were canted alarmingly and seemed to be on the verge of falling into the ordure, but even with these he found it hard to set aside the impression that they were watching him.

There was, he realized slowly, a reason for this absurd, frightening feeling. The totems testified to something more than the deaths of uncountable thousands of Chandalese. They were witness also to the fact that this gulf was known and visited, at least by the priest-chief caste; obviously the driving of the poles in this abyss was the final ritual act of condemnation of a city-state. He was not safe from pursuit yet.

And what, he found himself wondering despite his desperation, could it possibly be all about—this completely deliberate, systematic slaughter of whole nations of one's fellow beings by pestilence contrived and abetted? It was certainly not a form of warfare; *that* he might have understood. It was more like the extermination of the rabbits of Australia by infecting them with a plague. He remembered very dimly that the first settlers of North America had tried, unsuccessfully, to spread smallpox among the Indians for the same reason; but the memory seemed to be no help in understanding Chandala.

Again he heard that rhythmic sound, now much closer, and something large and peculiarly rubbery went by him, almost on a level with his shoulders. At his sudden movement, it rose and perched briefly on one of the totems, just too far ahead in the mist to be clearly visible.

He had not the slightest desire to get any closer to it, but the current was carrying him that way. As he approached, dragging the blade of the spear fruitlessly, the thing seemed to fall off the pole, and with a sudden flap of wings—he could just make out their spread, which seemed to be about four feet—disappeared into the murk.

He touched his gun. It did not reassure him much. It occurred to him that since this sea was visited, anything that lived here might hesitate to attack him, but he knew he could not count on that. The Chandalese might well have truces with such creatures which would not protect Naysmith for an instant. It was imperative to keep going, and if possible, to get out.

The totem poles were beginning to thin out. He could see high-water marks on the remaining ones, which meant that the underground ocean was large enough to show tides, but he had no idea what size that indicated; for one thing, he knew neither the mass nor the distance of Chandala's moon. He did remember, however, that he had seen no tide marks as he had entered the forest of idols, which meant that it was ebbing now; and it seemed to him that the current was distinctly faster than before.

He poled forward vigorously. Several times he heard the flapping noise and the fluttering sounds again, and not these alone. There were other noises. Some of them were impossible to interpret, and some of them so suggestive that he could only pray that he was wrong about them. For a while he tried shutting the radio off, but he found the silence inside the helmet even less possible to endure, as well as cutting him off from possible cues to pursuit.

But the current continued to pick up, and shortly he noticed that he was casting a shadow into the shell before him. If the source of the light, whatever it was, was over the centre of the sea, it was either relatively near the water or he had come a long distance; perhaps both.

Then there was a wall looming to his left side. Five more

long thrusts with the spear, and there was another on his right. The light dimmed; the water ran faster.

He was back on a river again. By the time the blackness closed down the current was rushing, and once more he was forced to sit down and use the spear as a steering oar. Again ahead of him he heard the scream of gas jets.

Mixed with that sound was another noise, a prolonged roaring which at first completely baffled him. Then, suddenly, he recognized it; it was the sound of a great cataract.

Frantically, he flashed his light about. There was a ledge of sorts beside the torrent, but he was going so fast now that to make a leap for it would risk smashing his helmet. All the same, he had no choice. He thrust the skidding coracle towards the wall and jumped.

He struck fair, on his feet. He secured his balance in time to see the shell swept away, with his pack and spare oxygen bottles.

For a reason he cannot now explain, this amused him.

This, as Naysmith chooses to tell it, is the end of the meaningful part of the story, though by no means the end of his travails; these he dismisses as "scenery". As his historian, I can't be quite so offhand about them, but he has supplied me with few details to go by.

He found the cataract, not very far ahead; evidently, he had jumped none too soon. As its sound had suggested, it was a monster, leaping over an underground cliff which he guesses must have been four or five miles high, into a cavern which might have been the Great Gulf itself. He says, and I think he is right, that we now have an explanation for the low density of Chandala: If the rest of it has as much underground area as the part he saw, its crust must be extremely porous. By this reckoning, the Chandalese underworld must have almost the surface area of Mars.

It must have seemed a world to itself indeed to Naysmith, standing on the rim of that gulf and looking down at its fire-filled floor. Where the cataract struck, steam rose in huge billows and plumes, and with a scream which forced him to shut off the radio at once. Occasionally the ground shook faintly under his feet.

Face to face with Hell, Naysmith found reason to hope. This inferno, it seemed to him, might well underlie the region of hot springs, geysers, and fumaroles towards which he had been heading from the beginning; and if so, there should be dead volcanic funnels through which he might escape to the surface. This proved to be the case; but first he had to pick his way around the edge of the abyss to search for one, starting occasional rockslides, the heat blasting through his helmet, and all in the most profound and unnatural silence. *If this is scenery, I prefer not to be offered any more scenic vacations.*

"But on the way, I figured it out," Naysmith told me. "Rituals don't grow without a reason—especially not rituals involving a whole culture. This one has a reason that I should have been the first to see—or any physician should. You, too."

"Thanks. But I *don't* see it. If the Heart stars do, they aren't telling."

"They must think it's obvious," Naysmith said. "It's eugenics. Most planets select for better genes by controlling breeding. The Chandalese do it by genocide. They force their lower castes to kill themselves off."

"Ugh. Are you sure? Is it scientific? I don't see how it could be, under the circumstances."

"Well, I don't have all the data. But I think a really thorough study of Chandalese history, with a statistician to help, would show that it is. It's also an enormously dangerous method, and it may wind up with the whole planet dead; that's the chance they're taking, and I assume they're aware of it."

"Well," I said, "assuming that it does work, I wouldn't admit a planet that 'survived' by that method into any federation *I* ran."

"No," Naysmith said soberly. "Neither would I. And there's the rub, you see, because the Heart stars *will*. That's what shook me. I may have been a lousy doctor—and don't waste your breath denying it, you know what I mean—but I've been giving at least lip service to all our standard humanitarian assumptions all my life, without ever examining them. What the Chandalese face up to, and we don't, is that death is now and has always been *the* drive wheel of evolution. They not only face up to it, they *use* it.

"When I was down there in the middle of that sewer, I was in the middle of my own *Goetzendaemmerung*—the twilight of the idols that Nietzsche speaks of. I could see all the totems of my own world, of my own life, falling into the muck . . . shooting like logs over the brink into Hell. And it was then that I knew I couldn't be a surgeon any more."

"Come now," I said. "You'll get over it. After all, it's just another planet with strange customs. There are millions of them."

"You weren't there," Naysmith said, looking over my shoulder at nothing. "For you, that's all it is. For me . . . 'No other taste shall change this.' Don't you see? All planets are Chandalas. It's not just that Hell is real. The laws that run it are the laws of life everywhere."

His gaze returned to me. It made me horribly uneasy.

"What was it Mephistopheles said? 'Why, this is Hell, nor am I out of it.' The totems are falling all around us as we sit here. One by one, Rosenbaum; one by one."

And that is how we lost Naysmith. It would have been easy enough to say simply that he had a desperate experience on a savage planet and that it damaged his sanity, and let it go at that. But it would not be true. I would dismiss it that way myself if I could.

But I cannot bring myself to forget that the Heart stars classify Chandala as a civilized world.

121

None so Blind

A number of readers, including Fritz Leiber, complained on its first appearance that this story wasn't a fantasy at all. But there are, on the contrary, two fantastic assumptions buried in it, one large and one small. The present title—which was the original, though not the one under which it first appeared—probably won't help, since the whole quotation from which it comes appeared in the magazine editor's blurb for the piece.

The early Mott Street morning was misty, but that would burn off later; it was going to be a hot day in New York. The double doors of the boarded-up shop swung inward with a grating noise, and a black-and-white tomcat bolted out of an overflowing garbage can next door and slid beneath a parked car. It was safe there: The car had been left in distress two days ago, and since then the neighbourhood kids had removed three tyres and the engine.

After that, nothing moved for a while. At last, a preternaturally clean old man, neatly dressed in very clean rags, came out of the dark, chill interior of the shop with a kettle heaped with freshly fired charcoal, which he set on the sidewalk. Straightening, he took a good long look at the day, exposing his cleanliness, the sign of his reclamation from the Bowery two blocks away, to the unkind air. Then he scuffled back into the cave with a bubbly sigh; he would next see the day tomorrow morning at the same time, if it didn't rain. Behind him, the bucket of charcoal sent up petals of yellow flame, in the midst of which the briquettes nestled like dragon's eggs, still unhatched.

Now emerged the hot-dog wagons, three of them, one by one, their blue-and-orange-striped parasols bobbing stiffly, pushed by men in stiff caps. The men helped themselves to charcoal from the bucket, to heat the franks (all meat) and the sauerkraut (all cabbage) and the rolls (all sawdust). Behind them came the fruit pushcarts, and then two carts heaped with the vegetables of the district: minute artichokes for three cents each, Italian tomatoes, eggplants in all sizes, zucchini, peppers, purple onions.

When the pushcarts were all gone the street was quiet again, but the cat stayed underneath the late-model wreck at the curb. It was waiting for the dogs, who after a while emerged with their men: scrubby, yellowing animals with long foxy noses and plumy tails carried low, hitched to the men with imaginative networks of old imitation-alligator belts and baby-carriage straps. There was also one authentic German shepherd who wore an authentic rigid Seeing-Eye harness; the man he was pulling was a powerfully built Negro who was already wearing his sign:

> PRAY IN YOUR OWN WAY
> EVERY DAY
>
> TAKE A PRAYER CARD
> THEY'RE FREE
> I AM BLIND
> THANK YOU

The others still carried their signs under their arms, though all were wearing their dark glasses. They paused to sniff at the day.

"Pretty good," said the man with the German shepherd. "Let's go. And don't any of you bastards be late back."

The others mumbled, and then they too filed off towards Houston Street, where the bums were already in motion towards the Volunteers of America shop, hoping to pick up a little heavy lifting to buy cigarettes with. The bums avoided the dogs very scrupulously. The dogs pulled the men west and down the sixty steps of the Broadway-Lafayette IND station to the F train, which begins there, and they all sat together in the rear car. There was almost no talking, but one of the men already had his transistor radio going, filling the car with a hysterical mixture of traffic reports and rock-and-roll.

The cat stayed under the late-model wreck; it was now time for the children to burst out of the church and charge towards the parochial school across the street, screaming and pummelling each other with their prayer books.

Another clean old man took in the empty charcoal bucket, and the doors closed.

The dogs pulled the men out of the F train at the Forty-seventh–Fiftieth Street station on Sixth Avenue, which is the Rockefeller Centre stop; they emerged, however, at the Forty-seventh Street end, which is almost squarely in the middle of Manhattan's diamond mart. Here they got out their cups, each of which contained a quarter to shake, and hung on their signs; then they moved singly, at five-minute intervals, one block north, and then slowly east.

The signs were all metal, hung at belt level, front and back, and all were black with greenish-yellow lettering. The calligraphy was also all the same: curlicue capitals, like the upper case of that type font known as Hobo.

The messages, however, were varied, though they had obvious similarities in style. The one following the man with the German shepherd and the prayer cards, for instance, said:

GOD BLESS YOU
YOU CAN SEE
AND I CAN'T
THANK YOU

Slowly they deployed along Forty-eighth Street towards Fifth Avenue, which was already teeming with people, though it was only 10 a.m. At the Fifth Avenue end, which is marked by Black, Starr and Gorham, a phenomenally expensive purveyor of such luxuries as one-fork-of-a-kind sterling, an old blind woman in the uniform of the Lighthouse sat behind a table on which was a tambourine, playing a guitar and whining out a hymn. A dog lay at her feet. Only a few feet away, still in front of one of Black, Starr and Gorham's show windows, was a young man with a dog, standing with a guitar, singing rock-and-roll at the top of his voice. Two blocks up Fifth Avenue, at the terrace of Rockefeller Centre, two women and a man in Salvation Army uniforms played hymns on three trumpets in close harmony (a change from yesterday, when that stand had been occupied only by an Army officer with a baritone saxhorn which he could barely play), but they didn't matter —the men weren't working Rockefeller Centre any more, having already done for that area.

The dogs ignored the old woman and the rock-and-roller as well, and so did the men. They never sang. The man with the transistor radio turned it up a little when he worked that end of the block.

The street filled still further. As it got on towards a blistering noon, the travellers that counted came out: advertising agency account men ("and when the client's sales forecast was under ours by fifteen per cent, they went and cut the budget on us, and now poor old Jim's got his yacht posted for sale in the men's room"), the middle echelons of editors from important weekly news magazines (with the latest dirty verses about their publishers), literary agents playing musical chairs ("went to S&S and took Zuck Stamler with him with twenty-five per cent of the contract and an option clause bound in purest brass"), and an occasional bewildered opinion-maker from the trade press ("a buck eighty-five for *spaghetti*?").

None of these ever dropped a coin in the cups, but the dogs were not disturbed; they walked their men in the heat.

None so Blind

I MAY SEE AGAIN
WITH A TRANSPLANT EYE
GOD BLESS YOU

The travellers settled in the St. Germain and the Three G's, except for the trade press, which took refuge in the American Bar. Secretaries stopped outside the restaurants, looked at the menus, looked at each other indignantly, and swung up Fifth towards Stouffer's, where they would be charged just as much. The match players said "Viva-la!" and "Law of averages!" and "That's a good call," and damned the Administration. The girl account exec had one Martini more and told the man from the client something he had suspected for five months and was not glad to hear; the agency would not be glad to hear it either, but it never would. Rogers and Whitehead, Authors Represent-atives (they had never been able to decide where the apostrophe should go), had shad roe and bacon and decided to drop all their Western authors, of whom they had three. The president and editor-in-chief of the largest magazine enterprise in the world decided to run for President after all.

The men listened and shook their cups and walked their dogs. The transistor radio reported that the news was worse today.

At 3 p.m. the temperature was 92 degrees, the humidity 40 per cent, the T.H.I. 80. The German shepherd pulled his man back towards Sixth. The other dogs followed. At the token booth the cups were checked: There was enough money to get home on. Along Forty-eighth, the restaurants emptied, leaving behind a thick miasma of smoke, tomato sauce, and disastrous decisions. Tomorrow they would do for Forty-seventh Street, where the public-relations types gathered.

The cave on Mott Street was relatively cool. The men took off their signs and sat down. The radio said something

126

about Khrushchev, something about Cuba, and something about beer.

"Not a bad day," the big man said finally. "Lots of jangle. Did you hear that guy with the three kids decide to quit?"

The man with the radio reported: "Goin' to rain tomorrow."

"It *is*?" the big man said. "Hell, that's no good." He thought for a while, and then, getting deliberately to his feet, he crossed the dark, chill room and kicked the German shepherd. "Who's in charge here?" The dog looked back sullenly. Satisfied, the man went back and sat down.

"Nah," he said. "It won't rain."

No Jokes on Mars

This story has several important features in common with
my novel *Welcome to Mars!* (1967), but neither depends
upon a knowledge of the other. Though the story was
written first, the events in it presumably take place at
least a decade after those in the novel.

The skimmer soared easily through a noon sky as blue-black
as freshly spilled washable ink. On Mars, the gravity was
so low that almost anything could be made to fly, given
power to spare; on Earth, the skimmer would have been
about as airworthy as a flat stone.

On Earth, Karen had never felt very airworthy either, but
here on Mars she weighed only forty-nine pounds and was
soaring nicely. She wished she could keep the Martian
weight when she got home, but she knew well enough that
the loss was only a loan.

The official strapped in on her right—as the first Earth-
side reporter in a year and a half, she had rated nothing
less than the executive officer of Port Ares—had already
shown signs of believing that Karen's weight was distributed
quite well, no matter what it was. That was pleasant, too.

"This is the true desert we're going over now—the real
Mars," he was saying, his voice muffled by his oxygen mask.
"That orange-red sand is hematite, a kind of iron ore. Like
most rusts, it's got a little water in it, and the Martian
lichens can get it out. Also, it can blow up a fine sandstorm."

Karen took no notes; she had known that much before

she'd left Cape Kennedy. Besides, perhaps perversely, she was more interested in Joe Kendricks, the skimmer's civilian pilot. Colonel Margolis was all right: young, hard-muscled, highly trained, with that modest but dedicated look cultivated by the Astronaut Corps. Like most of the A.C. complement here, he also looked as though he had spent most of his hitch at Port Ares under glass. Kendricks, on the other hand, looked weathered.

Joe Kendricks showed not the faintest sign of returning her interest. At the moment, his attention was totally on the skimmer and on the desert. He too was a reporter, representing a broadcasting-wire service pool, but since he had been on Mars since the second landing, he had suffered the usual fate of the local leg man: He had first become familiar, then invisible. Perhaps for this reason, or perhaps from simple staleness, or loneliness, or a combination of these and still other reasons, his copy lately had been showing signs of cynicism about the whole Mars venture.

Maybe that had been inevitable. All the same, when he had taken to slugging his weekly column "JoKe's on Mars", the home office emitted only one dutiful chuckle and sent Karen across forty-eight million miles of expensive space to trouble-shoot. Neither the press nor the A.C. wanted the taxpayer to think anybody found anything funny about Mars.

Kendricks banked the skimmer sharply and pointed down. "Cat," he said, to nobody in particular.

"Oho." Colonel Margolis picked up his binoculars. Karen followed suit. The glasses were difficult to look into through the eyepieces of her oxygen mask, and even more difficult to focus with the heavy gloves; but suddenly the big dune cat sprang to life in front of her.

It was beautiful. The dune cat, as all encyclopedias note, is the largest animal on Mars, usually measuring about four feet from nose to base of spine (it has no tail). The eyes, slitted and with an extra membrane against the flying sand, give it a vaguely catlike appearance, as does the calico pelt (orange, marbled with blue-green, which is actually a parasitic one-celled plant that helps supply its oxygen); but it is not a cat. Though it has an abdominal pouch like a kangaroo or a 'possum, it is not a marsupial either. Some of the encyclopedias—the cheaper and more sensational ones—suggest that it may be descended from the long-extinct Canal Masons of Mars, but since the Masons left behind neither pictures nor bones, this is at best only a wild guess.

It loped gracefully over the rusty dunes, heading in nearly a straight line, probably for the nearest oasis. Joe Kendricks followed it easily. Evidently, it hadn't yet spotted the skimmer, which was nearly noiseless in the Everest-thin air.

"A real break, Miss Chandler," Colonel Margolis was saying. "We don't see much action on Mars, but a cat's always good for a show. JoKe, have you got a spare canteen you can throw him?"

The leg man nodded and set his machine to wheeling in a wide arc over the cat, while Karen tried to puzzle out what Colonel Margolis could be talking about. Action? The only encyclopedia entry she recalled at all well said that the dune cat was "quick and strong, but aloof and harmless to man". Nobody, the entry added, knew what it ate.

Joe Kendricks produced a flat can of water, loosened the pull tab slightly, and, to Karen's astonishment—for water was worth more than fine gold on Mars—threw it over the side of the skimmer. It fell with dreamlike slowness in the weak gravity, but the weakened pull tab burst open when it struck, just ahead of the cat.

Instantly, the sands all around the cat were aswarm with creatures. They came running and wriggling towards the rapidly evaporating stain of water from as far away as fifteen feet.

Most of them were too small to be made out clearly, even through the binoculars. Karen was just as glad, for the two that she could see clearly were quite bad enough.

130

They were each about a foot long, and looked like a nightmare combination of centipede and scorpion. And where the other crawlers were all headed mindlessly towards the water stain, these had sensed that their first target had to be the dune cat.

The cat fought with silent fury, with great flat blows of one open paw; in the other, something metallic flashed in the weak, harsh sunlight. It paid no heed to the creatures' claws, though it sustained several bloody nips from them in the first few seconds; it was their stings it was wary of. Karen was instantly certain that they were venomous.

She was beginning to think the men in the skimmer were, too.

The struggle seemed to last forever, but it was actually only a moment before the cat had neatly amputated one sting, and had smashed the other horror halfway into the sand. From there it was upon the burst canteen with a single bound, and tossing back whatever trickle of liquid gold it might still hold.

Then, without a single upward glance, it was running like a dust devil for the near horizon. Nothing was left to see below but the smaller critters, some of which were now becoming aware of the two losers of the battle.

Karen discovered that she was breathing again—and that she had forgotten to take pictures. Colonel Margolis pounded Joe Kendricks excitedly on one shoulder.

"After him!" the A.C. officer crowed. "Let's not drop the ball now, JoKe. Give her the gun!"

Even beneath the oxygen mask there was something cold and withdrawn about the set of Kendricks' expression, but the skimmer nevertheless leapt obediently after the vanished dune cat. The cat was fast, but the chase was no contest.

"Set me down about a mile ahead of him," the colonel said. He loosened his pistol in its holster.

"Colonel," Karen said. "Are you—are you going to kill the cat? Even after the fight it put up?"

"No, indeed," Colonel Margolis said heartily. "Just collect our little fee for the water we gave it. Over behind that dune looks about right, JoKe."

"It isn't legal," Kendricks said unexpectedly. "You know that."

"The law's an anachronism," the colonel said in an even voice. "Hasn't been enforced for years."

"You should know," Kendricks said. "You enforce 'em. All right, hop out. I'll cover you."

The A.C. officer jumped from the hovering skimmer to the rusty sand, and Kendricks took the machine aloft again, circling him.

The cat stopped when it topped the rise and saw the man, but after a glance aloft at the skimmer, it did not try to run away. The colonel had his gun out now, but he was not pointing it anywhere.

"I should very much like to know," Karen said in her quietest and most dangerous voice, "just exactly what is going on here."

"A little quiet poaching," Kendricks said, his eyes on the ground. "The cat carries a thing in his pouch. Our hero down there is going to rob him of it."

"But—what is it? Is it valuable?"

"Valuable to the cat, but valuable enough to the colonel. Ever seen a Martian pomander?"

Karen had indeed seen several; they had been the ultimate in gifts from swains for several years. It was a fuzzy sphere about the size of a grape, which, when suspended and warmed between the breasts, surrounded the wearer with a sweet and literally unearthly musk. Karen had tried one only once, for the perfume, though light, also had a faint narcotic quality which encouraged a lady to say "maybe" when what she had meant was "no".

"The pomander—it's part of the cat? Or a charm or treasure or something like that?"

"Well, that's hard to say. The experts call it his hibernation organ—he won't get through next winter without it. It isn't attached to him in any way, but the cats always act as though they can't come by another one—or grow another, whichever it is."

Karen clenched her fists. "Joe—put me down."

He darted a quick sidewise glance at her. "I wouldn't advise it. There's nothing you can do—and I know. I've tried."

"Joe Kendricks, I don't know what else you'd call what's going on down there, but there's one thing you know it is, as well as I do. It's a story—and I want it."

"You'll never get it off the planet," he said. "But—all right, all right. Down we go."

As they trudged closer, the cat, erect, seemed to be holding out something towards the colonel, who had his back to them. Because it was closer to the crest of the dune than the man was, the cat did not seem to be any shorter. After a moment, Colonel Margolis threw back his head and laughed. At this distance the air failed to carry the sound.

"Not the pomander," Joe Kendricks muttered without waiting for Karen's question. "It's trying to buy its life with a shard. They always do."

"What's——?"

"A stone with Canal Mason inscriptions on it."

"But Joe! Surely *that's* valuable!"

"Not worth a dime; the planet's littered with them. The Masons wrote all over every brick they laid. The cat could have picked that one up right where he's standing. Nobody's ever been able to read a line of the stuff, anyhow. No connection to Earthly languages."

The cat saw them now; it turned slightly and held out its fragment of stone towards Joe Kendricks. Colonel Margolis looked at them over his shoulder with a start of annoyance.

"No good, cat," he said harshly. "It's *me* you're dickering with. And I don't want your rock. Empty the pouch."

133

He could not possibly have expected the dune cat to understand his words—but the situation, and a brusque eviscerating gesture of both his hands, obviously had already conveyed more than enough.

Another slight movement, and slanted eyes like twin sapphires blazed into Karen's own out of the tigerish mask. In a gnarled voice that carried human speech only with pain, the dune cat said:

"Missessss Earsssman, buy?"

It held out the worthless bit of brick it offered for its life. Its stare was proud, and its out-thrust paw absolutely steady.

"I'll be glad to buy," Karen said, and reached out. "And, Colonel Margolis—the Lord and the Astronaut Corps help you if you break my bargain."

Gloved hand touched orange paw. The Martian looked at her a moment longer, and then was gone.

Colonel Margolis remained silent during the whole of the trip back to Port Ares, but once there, he lost no time in having them both on the carpet—in, of course, his own office. He was obviously also in a pet—in part, Karen was almost sure, for having made up to her in the first place. *Well, that's the way the world wags, Colonel; actions have consequences . . . even on Mars.*

"It won't be possible for me to behave as if this hadn't happened," he said, in a voice intended to convey good will. "The cats are smart enough to spread the word, and it'll take months to pound home to them that your behaviour doesn't mean anything. But if I can have your promise not to say anything further about it, at least I won't be forced to have you shipped home by the next rocket."

"Five months from now," Joe Kendricks added helpfully.

"It had better mean something, and it'd better be just the beginning," Karen said. "Do you think women would go on using these pomanders if they knew what they were—and what they cost? This story's going to be told."

There was a brief silence. Then Kendricks said: "One story doesn't make a scandal."

"Not even with the base commander in the middle of it?"

But the colonel only smiled gently. "I don't mind being a villain, if the colony needs one," he said. "You can hang me by my thumbs if you like. I'd be interested to see how many people back home take your word against mine, though."

"I've never pilloried anybody in my life, and my editors know it," Karen said. "But that's a long way from the point. It isn't just one story. It's the pomander trade as a whole that's the scandal."

The colonel abruptly turned his back and looked out of the window at the domed colony—a spectacle of struggle against a terrible world, a vast planetary desert about which Karen knew she knew very little. He said: "All right, I tried. Now it's your turn, JoKe. Set her straight."

"Don't call me that," Kendricks growled. Then: "But Miss Chandler, the Corps isn't going to let you stop the pomander trade—don't you know that? It's supposed to be immune even from petty graft. And this is far from petty. If the law's been broken—and God knows it has—half the men in Port Ares have a slice of the profits. It can't be stopped now."

"All the worse," Karen said. "But we can stop it, Joe; you can help me. They can't ship both of us home."

"Don't you think I've tried to get this story off Mars before?" Kendricks said angrily. "The Corps 'reviews' every line that leaves the planet. After this incident, the colonel here will read my copy himself——"

"You bet," Colonel Margolis said, with a certain relish.

"—and I've got to live with this crew the year around." After a moment, Kendricks added, "Six hundred and sixty-eight days a year."

"That's just why they can't kill the story in the long run,"

Karen said eagerly. "If they're censoring you, you can slip the word to me somehow, sooner or later. I know how to read between the lines—and you know how to write between them. The censor doesn't exist who's awake every second!"

"They can kill me," Joe Kendricks said stolidly. "Both of us, if they have to. The next ship home is five months away, and people get killed on Mars all the time."

Karen let fly an unladylike snort. "JoKe, you're scared. Do you think a Corps commandant would kill the only two reporters on Mars? How would *that* look in his record, no matter how careful he was?"

Colonel Margolis turned back to glare at them. But when he spoke, his voice was remarkably neutral.

"Look, let's be reasonable," he said. "Why so much fuss over one small irregularity, when there's so much being accomplished on Mars that's positive, that's downright great? This is one of humanity's greatest outposts. Why spoil it for the sake of a sensation? Why not just live and let live?"

"Because that's just what you're *not* doing," Karen said. "You told me that you weren't going to kill the cat this afternoon, but you didn't tell me it would die later, in the winter, when you were through stealing from it. It's the Spaniards and the Incas all over again! Are we spending billions to reach the planets, just to export the same old crimes against the natives?"

"Now, calm down a minute, please, Miss Chandler. The cats are only animals. You're exaggerating a good deal, you know."

"I don't think she is," Joe Kendricks said in a low voice. "The dune cats are intelligent. Killing them off is criminal— I've always thought so, and so does the law. Karen, I'll try to get the dope out to you, but the Corps has the manpower here to stop me if it really tries. I may have to bring the rest of the story back to Earth with me, instead—a matter of years. Can you wait that long?"

They looked at each other for a long moment. His expression was much changed.

Karen said: "You bet I'll wait."

He drew a deep breath. "You're sure you mean that?"

"Dead sure, Joe," Karen said. "The jokes are over."

How Beautiful with Banners

A good many years ago, Damon Knight discovered that —unbeknownst to me—two early stories of mine were heavily loaded with symbols; and that these symbols showed that the stories, despite quite different overt contents, were about the same basic theme. When Damon later asked me to write a story for the first issue of his book-magazine *Orbit*, I thought it appropriate to give the piece such a symbol system consciously, and this is the result.

Feeling as naked as a peppermint soldier in her transparent film wrap, Dr. Ulla Hillström watched a flying cloak swirl away towards the black horizon with a certain consequent irony. Although nearly transparent itself in the distant dim arc-light flame that was Titan's sun, the fluttering creature looked warmer than what she was wearing, for all that reason said it was at the same minus 316° F. as the thin methane it flew in. Despite the virus space-bubble's warranted and eerie efficiency, she found its vigilance—itself probably as close to alive as the flying cloak was—rather difficult to believe in, let alone to trust.

The machine—as Ulla much preferred to think of it—was inarguably an improvement on the old-fashioned pressure suit. Fashioned (or more accurately, cultured) of a single colossal protein molecule, the vanishingly thin sheet of life-stuff processed gases, maintained pressure, monitored radiation through almost the whole of the electromagnetic spectrum, and above all did not get in the way. Also, it could not be cut, punctured, or indeed sustain any damage short

138

of total destruction; macroscopically, it was a single, primary unit, with all the physical integrity of a crystal of salt or steel.

If it did not actually think, Ulla was grateful; often it almost seemed to, which was sufficient. Its primary drawback for her was that much of the time it did not really seem to be there.

Still, it seemed to be functioning; otherwise, Ulla would in fact have been as solid as a stick of candy, toppled forever across the confectionery whiteness that frosted the knife-edge stones of this cruel moon, layer upon layer. Outside—only a perilous few inches from the lightly clothed warmth of her skin—the brief gust the cloak had been soaring on died, leaving behind a silence so cataleptic that she could hear the snow creaking in a mockery of motion. Impossible though it was to comprehend, it was getting still colder out there; Titan was swinging out across Saturn's orbit towards eclipse, and the apparently fixed sun was secretly going down, its descent sensed by the snows no matter what her Earthly eyes, accustomed to the nervousness of living skies, tried to tell her. In another two Earth days it would be gone, for an eternal week.

At the thought, Ulla turned to look back the way she had come that morning. The virus bubble flowed smoothly with the motion, and the stars became brighter as it compensated for the fact that the sun was now at her back. She still could not see the base camp, of course. She had come too far for that, and in any event it was wholly underground except for a few wiry palps, hollowed out of the bitter rock by the blunt-nosed ardour of prolapse drills; the repeated nannosecond birth and death of primordial ylem the drills had induced while that cavern was being imploded had seemed to convulse the whole demon womb of this world, but in the present silence the very memory of the noise seemed false.

Now there was no sound but the creaking of the methane

snow; and nothing to see but a blunt, faint spearhead of hazy light, deceptively like an Earthly aurora or the corona of the sun, pushing its way from below the edge of the cold into the indifferent company of the stars. Saturn's rings were rising, very slightly awaver in the dark-blue air, like the banners of a spectral army. The idiot face of the giant gas planet itself, faintly striped with meaningless storms as though trying to remember a childhood passion, would be glaring down at her before she could get home if she didn't get herself in motion soon. Obscurely disturbed, Dr. Hillström faced front and began to unlimber her sled.

The touch and clink of the instruments cheered her a little, even in this ultimate loneliness. She was efficient—many years, and a good many suppressed impulses had seen to that; it was too late for temblors, especially so far out from the sun that had warmed her Stockholm streets and her silly friendships. All those null-adventures were gone now like a sickness. The phantom embrace of the virus suit was perhaps less satisfying—only *perhaps*—but it was much more reliable. Much more reliable; she could depend on that.

Then, as she bent to thrust the spike of a thermocouple into the wedding-cake soil, the second flying cloak (or was it that same one?) hit her in the small of the back and tumbled her into nightmare.

2

With the sudden darkness there came a profound, ambiguous emotional blow—ambiguous, yet with something shockingly familiar about it. Instantly exhausted, she felt herself go flaccid and unstrung, and her mind, adrift in nowhere, blurred and spun downward too into the swamps of trance.

The long fall slowed just short of unconsciousness, lodged precariously upon a shelf of a dream, a mental buttress founded four years in the past—a long distance, when one recalls that in a four-dimensional plenum every second of time is one hundred eighty-six thousand miles of space—and eight hundred millions of miles away. The memory was curiously inconsequential to have arrested her, let alone supported her: not of her home, of her few triumphs, or even of her aborted marriage, but of a sordid little encounter with a reporter that she had talked herself into at the Madrid genetics conference, when she herself had already been an associate professor, a Swedish Government delegate, a twenty-five-year-old divorcee, and altogether a woman who should have known better.

But better than what? The life of science even in those days had been almost by definition the life of the eternal campus exile; there was so much to learn—or, at least, to show competence in—that people who wanted to be involved in the ordinary, vivid concerns of human beings could not stay with it long, indeed often could not even be recruited; they turned aside from the prospect with a shudder, or even a snort of scorn. To prepare for the sciences had become a career in indefinitely protracted adolescence, from which one awakened fitfully to find one's self spending a one-night stand in the body of a stranger. It had given her no pride, no self-love, no defences of any sort; only a queer kind of virgin numbness, highly dependent upon familiar surroundings and valueless habits, and easily breached by any normally confident siege in print, in person, anywhere—and remaining just as numb as before when the seizure of fashion, politics, or romanticism had swept by and left her stranded, too easy a recruit to have been allowed into the centre of things or even considered for it.

Curious—most curious—that in her present remote terror she should find even a moment's rest upon so wobbling a pivot. The Madrid incident had not been important; she had been through with it almost at once. Of course, as she had often told herself, she had never been promiscuous, and

141

had often described the affair, defiantly, as that one (or at worst, second) test of the joys of impulse which any woman is entitled to have in her history. Nor had it really been that joyous: She could not now recall the boy's face, and remembered how he had felt primarily because he had been in so casual and contemptuous a hurry.

But now that she came to dream of it, she saw with a bloodless, lightless eye that all her life, in this way and in that, she had been repeatedly seduced by the inconsequential. She had nothing else to remember even in this hour of her presumptive death. Acts have consequences, a thought told her, but not ours; we have done, but never felt. We are no more alone on Titan, you and I, than we have ever been. *Basta, per carita!*—so much for Ulla.

Awakening in this same darkness as before, Ulla felt the virus bubble snuggling closer to her blind skin, and recognized the shock that had so regressed her: a shock of recognition, but recognition of something she had never felt herself. Alone in a Titanic snowfield, she had eavesdropped on an . . .

No. Not possible. Sniffling, and still blind, she pushed the cozy bubble away from her breasts and tried to stand up. Light flushed briefly around her, as though the bubble had cleared just above her forehead and then clouded again. She was still alive, but everything else was utterly problematical. What had happened to her? She simply did not know.

Therefore, she thought, begin with ignorance. No one begins anywhere else . . . but I didn't know even that, once upon a time.

Hence:

3

Though the virus bubble ordinarily regulated itself, there was a control box on her hip—actually an ultrashort-range microwave transmitter—by which it could be modulated, against more special environments than the bubble itself could cope with alone. She had never had to use it before, but she tried it now.

The fogged bubble cleared patchily, but it would not stay cleared. Crazy moires and herringbone patterns swept over it, changing direction repeatedly, and outside the snowy landscape kept changing colour like a delirium. She found, however, that by continuously working the frequency knob on her box—at random, for the responses seemed to bear no relation to the Braille calibrations on the dial—she could maintain outside vision of a sort in pulses of two or three seconds each.

This was enough to show her, finally, what had happened. There was a flying cloak around her. This in itself was unprecedented; the cloaks had never attacked a man before, or indeed paid any of them the least attention during their brief previous forays. On the other hand, this was the first time anyone had ventured more than five or ten minutes outdoors in a virus suit.

It occurred to her suddenly that in so far as anything was known about the nature of the cloaks, they were in some respects much like the bubbles. It was almost as though the one were a wild species of the other.

It was an alarming notion and possibly only a trope, containing as little truth as most poetry. Annoyingly, she found herself wondering if, once she got out of this mess, the men at the base camp would take to referring to it as "the cloak and suit business".

The snowfield began to turn brighter; Saturn was rising. For a moment the drifts were a pale straw colour, the normal hue of Saturnlight through an atmosphere; then it turned a raving Kelly green. Muttering, Ulla twisted the potentiometer dial, and was rewarded with a brief flash of normal illumination which was promptly overridden by a torrent of crimson lake, as though she were seeing everything in terms of a series of lithographer's colour separations.

Since she could not help this, she clenched her teeth and ignored it. It was much more important to find out what the flying cloak had done to her bubble, if she were to have any hope of shucking the thing.

There was no clear separation between the bubble and the Titanian creature. They seemed to have blended into a mélange which was neither one nor the other, but a sort of coarse burlesque of both. Yet the total surface area of the integument about her did not seem to be any greater—only more ill-fitting, less responsive to her own needs. Not *much* less; after all, she was still alive, and any really gross insensitivity to the demands and cues of her body would have been instantly fatal; but there was no way to guess how long the bubble would stay even that obedient. At the moment the wild thing that had enslaved it was perhaps most like a bear sark, dangerous to the wearer only if she panicked, but the change might well be progressive, pointed ultimately towards some Saturnine equivalent of the shirt of Nessus.

And that might be happening very rapidly. She might not be allowed the time to think her way out of this fix by herself. Little though she wanted any help from the men at the base camp, and useless though she was sure they would prove, she'd damn well better ask for it now, just in case.

But the bubble was not allowing any radio transmission through its roiling unicell wall today. The earphone was dead; not even the hiss of the stars came through it—only an occasional pop of noise that was born of entropy loss in the circuits themselves.

She was cut off. *Nun denn, allein!*

With the thought, the bubble cloak shifted again around her. A sudden pressure at her lower abdomen made her stumble forward over the crisp snow, four or five steps. Then it was motionless once more, except within itself.

That it should be able to do this was not surprising, for the cloaks had to be able to flex voluntarily at least a little in order to catch the thermals they rode, and the bubble had to be able to vary its dimensions and surface tension over a wide range to withstand pressure changes, outside and in, and do it automatically. No, of course the combination would be able to move by itself; what was disquieting was that it should want to.

Another stir of movement in the middle distance caught her eye: a free cloak, seemingly riding an updraught over a fixed point. For a moment she wondered what on that ground could be warm enough to produce so localized a thermal. Then, abruptly, she realized that she was shaking with hatred, and fought furiously to drive the spasm down, her fingernails slicing into her naked palms.

A raster of jagged black lines, like a television interference pattern, broke across her view and brought her attention fully back to the minutely solipsistic confines of her dilemma. The wave of emotion, nevertheless, would not quite go away, and she had a vague but persistent impression that it was being imposed from outside, at least in part—a cold passion she was interpreting as fury because its real nature, whatever it was, had no necessary relevance to her own imprisoned soul. For all that it was her own life and no other that was in peril, she felt guilty, as though she was eavesdropping, and as angry with herself as with what she was overhearing; yet burning as helplessly as the forbidden lamp in the bedchamber of Psyche and Eros.

Another trope—but was it, after all, so far-fetched? She was a mortal present at the mating of inhuman essences; mountainously far from home; borne here like the invisible lovers upon the arms of the wind; empalaced by a whole virgin-white world, over which flew the banners of a high god and a father of gods; and, equally appropriately, Venus was very far away from whatever love was being celebrated here.

What ancient and coincidental nonsense! Next she would be thinking herself degraded at the foot of some cross.

Yet the impression, of an eerie tempest going on just slightly outside any possibility of understanding what it was, would not pass away. Still worse, it seemed to mean something, to be important, to mock her with subtle clues to matters of great moment, of which her own present trap was only the first and not necessarily the most significant.

And suppose that all these impressions were in fact not extraneous or irrelevant, but did have some import—not just as an abstract puzzle, but to that morsel of displaced life that was Ulla Hillström? She was certainly no Freudian —that farrago of poetry and tosh had been passé for so long that it was now hard to understand how anybody, let alone a whole era, had been bemused by it—but it was too late now to rule out the repulsive possibility. No matter how frozen her present world, she could not escape the fact that, from the moment the cloak had captured her, she had been equally ridden by a Sabbat of specifically erotic memories, images, notions, analogies, myths, symbols, and frank physical sensations, all the more obtrusive because they were both inappropriate and disconnected. It might well have to be faced that a season of love can fall due in the heaviest weather—and never mind the terrors that flow in with it, or what deep damnations. At the very least, it was possible that somewhere in all this was the clue that would help her to divorce herself at last even from this violent embrace.

But the concept was preposterous enough to defer consideration of it if there were any other avenues open, and at least one seemed to be: the source of the thermal. The virus bubble, like many of the Terrestrial micro-organisms to which it was analogous, could survive temperatures well above boiling, but it seemed reasonable to assume that the flying cloaks, evolved on a world where even words congealed, might be sensitive to a relatively slight amount of heat.

Now, could she move inside this shroud of her own volition? She tried a step. The sensation was tacky, as though she were ploughing in thin honey, but it did not impede her except for a slight imposed clumsiness which experience ought to obviate. She was able to mount the sled with no trouble.

The cogs bit into the snow with a dry, almost inaudible squeaking, and the sled inched forward. Ulla held it to as slow a crawl as possible, because of her interrupted vision.

The free cloak was still in sight, approximately where it had been before, in so far as she could judge against this featureless snowscape—which was fortunate, since it might well be her only flag for the source of the thermal, whatever it was.

A peculiar fluttering in her surroundings—a whisper of sound, of motion, of flickering in the light—distracted her. It was as though her compound sheath were trembling slightly. The impression grew slowly more pronounced as the sled continued to lurch forward. As usual, there seemed to be nothing she could do about it except, possibly, to retreat; but she could not do that either, now; she was committed. Outside, she began to hear the soft soughing of a steady wind.

The cause of the thermal, when she finally reached it, was almost bathetic: a pool of liquid. Placid and deep blue, it lay inside a fissure in a low, heart-shaped hummock, rimmed with feathery snow. It looked like nothing more or less than a spring, though she did not for a moment suppose that the liquid could be water. She could not see the bottom of it; evidently, it was welling up from a fair depth. The spring analogy was probably completely false; the existence of anything in a liquid state on this world had to be thought of as a form of vulcanism. Certainly the column of heat rising from it was considerable; despite the thinness of the air, the wind here nearly howled. The free cloak floated up and down, about a hundred feet above her, like the last leaf of a long, cruel autumn. Nearer home, the bubble cloak shook with something comically like subdued fury.

Now, what to do? Should she push boldly into that cleft, hoping that the alien part of the bubble cloak would be unable to bear the heat? Close up, that course now seemed foolish, as long as she was ignorant of the real nature of the magma down there. And, besides, any effective immersion would probably have to surround at least half of the total surface area of the bubble, which wasn't practicable—the well wasn't big enough to accommodate it, even supposing that the compromised virus suit did not fight back, as in the pure state it had been obligated to do. On the whole, she was reluctantly glad that the experiment was impossible, for the mere notion of risking a new immolation in that problematical hole gave her the horrors.

Yet the time left for decision was obviously now very short, even supposing—as she had no right to do—that the environment-maintaining functions of the suit were still in perfect order. The quivering of the bubble was close to being explosive, and even were it to remain intact, it might shut her off from the outside world at any second.

The free cloak dipped lower, as if in curiosity. That only made the trembling worse. She wondered why.

Was it possible—was it possible that the thing embracing her companion was jealous?

4

There was no time left to examine the notion, no time even to sneer at it. Act—act! Forcing her way off the sled, she stumbled to the mound and looked frantically for some way of stopping it up. If she could shut off the thermal, bring the free cloak still closer—but how?

Throw rocks. But were there any? Yes, there were two, not very big, but at least she could move them. She bent stiffly and tumbled them into the crater.

The liquid froze around them with soundless speed. In seconds, the snow rimming the pool had drawn completely over it, like lips closing, leaving behind only a faint dimpled streak of shadow on a white ground.

The wind moaned and died, and the free cloak, its hems outspread to the uttermost, sank down as if to wrap her in still another deadly swath. Shadow spread around her; the falling cloak, its colour deepening, blotted Saturn from the sky, and then was sprawling over the beautiful banners of the rings—

The virus bubble convulsed and turned black, throwing her to the frozen ground beside the hummock like a bead doll. A blast of wind squalled over her.

Terrified, she tried to curl into a ball. The suit puffed up around her.

Then at last, with a searing, invisible wrench at its contained kernel of space-time, which burned out the control box instantly, the single creature that was the bubble cloak tore itself free of Ulla and rose to join its incomplete fellow.

In the single second before she froze forever into the livid backdrop of Titan, she failed even to find time to regret what she had never felt; for she had never known it, and only died as she had lived, an artifact of successful calculation. She never saw the cloaks go flapping away downwind —nor could it ever have occurred to her that she had brought heterosexuality to Titan, thus beginning that long evolution the end of which, sixty millions of years away, no human being would see.

No; her last thought was for the virus bubble, and it was only three words long:

You goddam philanderer—

Almost on the horizon, the two cloaks, the two Titanians, flailed and tore at each other, becoming smaller and smaller with distance. Bits and pieces of them flaked off and fell down the sky like ragged tears. Ungainly though the cloaks normally were, they courted even more clumsily.

Beside Ulla, the well was gone; it might never have existed. Overhead, the banners of the rings flew changelessly, as though they too had seen nothing—or perhaps, as though in the last six billion years they had seen everything, siftings upon siftings in oblivion, until nothing remained but the banners of their own mirrored beauty.

Skysign

Pace the school of thought represented at its best by the late Anthony Boucher, which believes that only the brilliantly original science-fiction story has any reason for existing, it has always seemed to me that the best work in this field consists largely of stories which re-examine the basic fantasy premises—of which there are only a few—and try to take them seriously. The alternative is a chase after novelty which all too often results in nothing but a predictable trifle. Whatever the outcome in the present instance, I think everyone will recognize the core of the following story as one of the commonest of adolescent daydreams; the real question is, where does it go from there?

> "Und ein Schiff mit acht Segeln
> Und mit fuenfzig Kanonen
> Wird entschwinden mit mir."
>
> PIRATE-JENNY: *The Threepenny Opera*

1

Carl Wade came back to consciousness slowly and with a dull headachey feeling, as though fighting off a barbiturate hangover—as under the circumstances was quite possible. He remembered right away that he had been one of the people who had volunteered to go aboard the alien spaceship which had been hanging motionless over San Francisco for the last month. The "lay volunteer", the Pentagon men had insultingly called him. And it was likely that the aliens would have drugged him, because to them, after all, he was only a specimen, and therefore possibly dangerous—

151

But that didn't seem quite right. Somehow, he could not bring his memory into focus. He hadn't actually been taken aboard the ship, as far as he could recall. On the night before he had been supposed to join the volunteer group, in honour of his own approaching martyrdom (as he liked to think of it) he and some friends from the local Hobbit Society, including the new girl, had cycled up to Telegraph Hill to take a look at the great ship. But it had only just continued to hang there, showing no lights, no motion, no activity of any kind except a faint Moon-highlight, as had been the case ever since it had first popped into view in the skies over Berkeley—it responded only to the answers to its own radio messages, only to answers, never to questions—and the club had quickly gotten bored with it.

And then what? Had they all gone off and gotten drunk? Had he managed to get the new girl to bed and was now about to have one of those morning-afters beside her? Or was he in a cell as an aftermath of a fairy-kicking brawl?

No one of these ideas evoked any echo in his memory except old ones; and a persistent hunch that he *was* on the spaceship, all the same, discouraged him from opening his eyes yet. He wondered what insanity had ever led him to volunteer, and what even greater insanity had led the Pentagon people to choose him over all the saucerites and other space nuts.

A vague clink of sound, subdued and metallic, caught his attention. He couldn't identify it, but somehow it sounded surgical. As far as it went, this matched with the quiet around him, the clean coolness of the air, and the un-rumpled, also apparently clean pallet he seemed to be lying on. He was neither in a jail nor in the pad of anybody he knew. On the other hand, he didn't feel ill enough to be in a hospital ward; just a little drugged. The college infirmary? No, nonsense, he'd been thrown out of college last year.

In short, he *must* be on the ship, simply because this must be the day after yesterday. The thought made him squeeze

his eyes still tighter shut. A moment later, further speculation was cut off by a feminine voice, unknown to him, and
both pleasantly sexy and unpleasantly self-possessed, but
obviously human. It said:

"I see you've given us his language, rather than him ours."

"It cops out on—rules out—avoids—obviates making
everyone else on board guard their tongues," a man's voice
replied. "Man, I really had to dig for that one. He's got a
constipated vocabulary; knows words, but hates them."

"That's helpful, too," the woman's voice responded. "If
he can't address himself precisely, it'll matter less what *we*
say to him."

Man, Carl thought, if I ever get that chick where I want
her, I'll sell chances on her to wetbacks. But she was still
talking:

"But what's he faking for, Brand? He's obviously wide
awake."

At this Carl opened eyes and mouth to protest indignantly
that he wasn't faking, realized his mistake, tried to close
both again, and found himself gasping and goggling instead.

He could not see the woman, but the man called Brand
was standing directly over him, looking down into his face.
Brand looked like a robot—no; remembering the man's
snotty remark about his vocabulary, Carl corrected himself:
He looked like a fine silver statue, or like a silver version of
Talos, the Man of Brass (and wouldn't Carl's damned
faculty advisor have been surprised at how fast he'd come up
with that one!). The metal shone brilliantly in the blue light
of the surgery-like room, but it did not look like plate metal.
It did not look hard at all. When Brand moved, it flowed
with the movement of the muscles under it, like skin.

Yet somehow Carl was dead sure that it wasn't skin, but
clothing of some sort. Between the metallic eye-slits, the
man's eyes were brown and human, and Carl could even see
the faint webbing of blood-vessels in their whites. Also,
when he spoke, the inside of his mouth was normal mucous

membrane—black like a chow's mouth instead of red, but certainly not metal. On the other hand, the mouth, disconcertingly, vanished entirely when it was closed, and so did the eyes when they blinked; the metal flowed together as instantly as it parted.

"That's better," the man said. "Check his responses, Lavelle. He still looks a little dopey. Damn this language."

He turned away and the woman—her name had certainly sounded like Lavelle—came into view, obviously in no hurry. She was metallic, too, but her metal was black, though her eyes were grey-green. The integument was exceedingly like a skin, yet seeing her, Carl was even more convinced that it was either clothing or a body-mask, for there was nothing at all to see where Carl instantly looked. Also, he noticed a moment later, either she had no hair or else her skull-cap—if that was what she wore—was very tight, a point that hadn't occurred to him while looking at the man.

She took Carl's pulse, and then looked expertly under his upper eyelids. "Slight fugue, that's all," she said with a startling pink flash of tongue. Yet not quite so startling as Brand's speaking had been, since a pink mouth in a black face was closer to Carl's experience than was any sort of mouth in a silver face. "He can go down to the cages any time."

Cages?

"Demonstration first," Brand, now out of sight again, said in an abstracted voice. Carl chanced moving his head slightly, and found that his horizon-headache was actually a faint, one-sided earache, which made no sense to him at all. The movement also showed him the dimensions of the room, which was no larger than an ordinary living-room—maybe twelve feet by thirteen feet—and painted an off-white. There was also some electronic apparatus here and there, but no more than Carl had seen in the pads of some hi-fi bugs he knew, and to his eyes not much more interesting. In a corner was a drop-down bunk, evidently duplicating the one he now occupied. Over an oval metal door—the only ship-like feature he could see—was a dial-face like that of a large barometer or clock, its figures too small to read from where he lay, and much too closely spaced, too.

Brand reappeared. After a moment, the shining black woman called Lavelle took up a position a few feet behind him and to his left.

"I want to show you something," the man said to Carl. "You can see just by looking at us that it would do you no good to jump us—to attack us. Do you dig—do you understand that?"

"Sure," Carl said, rather more eagerly than he had intended. As a first word, it wasn't a very good one.

"All right." Brand put both hands on his hips, just below his waist, and seemed to brace himself slightly. "But there's a lot more to it than you see at the moment. Watch closely."

Instantly, the silver man and Lavelle changed places. It happened so suddenly and without any transition that for a second Carl failed to register what he was supposed to have noticed. Neither of the two metal people had moved in the slightest. They were just each one standing where the other one had been standing before.

"Now——" the man said.

At once, he was back where he had been, but the gleaming black woman—man, that outfit was sexy!—was standing far back, by the oval door. Again, there'd been not a whisper or hint of any motion in the room.

"And once more——"

This time, the result was much more confusing. The metal aliens seemed to have moved, but after a while Carl realized that they hadn't; *he* had. The switch was so drastic that for an instant he had thought they—all three of them—were in another room; even the hands of the dial-face looked changed. But actually, all that had happened was that he was now in the other bunk.

The switch made hash of a hypothesis he had only barely begun to work out: that the metal skins or suits made it possible for Brand and Lavelle to swap places, or jump elsewhere at will, by something like teleportation. If that was how it worked, then Carl might just hook one of those shiny suits, and then, *flup*! and—

—and without benefit of suit white or black, he was in the other bunk, huddled in the ruins of his theory and feeling damned scared. On the face of a cathode-ray oscilloscope now in his field of view, a wiggly green trace diagrammed pulses which he was sure showed exactly how scared he was; he had always suspected any such instrument of being able to read his mind. The suspicion turned to rage and humiliation when Lavelle looked at the machine's display and laughed, in a descending arpeggio, like a coloratura soprano.

"He draws the moral," she said.

Wetbacks. Also King Kong, if possible.

"Possibly," said the silver man. "We'll let it go for now, anyhow. It's time for the next subject. You can get up now."

This last sentence seemed to be addressed to Carl. He stiffened for a moment, half expecting either the metal people or the room—or perhaps himself—to vanish, but since nothing at all changed, he slid cautiously to his feet.

Looking down at the feet, and on upward from there as far as he could without seeming vain about it, he discovered that he was wearing the same scuffed sneakers and soiled slacks he had been wearing when he had gone cycling with the Hobbit crowd, except that both the clothing and his own self under it had been given a thorough bath. He was offended by the discovery, but at the moment not very much. Did it mean that there really had been *no* events between that expedition to Telegraph Hill, and this nightmare?

"Am I on the ship?" he said. It was a difficult sentence to get out.

"Of course," said the silver man.

156

"But I never got to join the official party—or I don't think——"

"Nobody will come aboard with the official party, Jack. We selected the few we wanted from among the cats your people designated. The rest will cool their heels."

"Then what am I——"

"Too many answers," Lavelle said.

"Never mind," said the silver man. "It won't matter for long, chicklet. Come along, Mister—Wade?—yes; we'll interview you later, and answer some of your questions then, if we feel up to it. Lavelle, stay here and set up for the next live one. And Mister Wade, one other thing. Should you feel ambitious, just bear in mind——"

The metal-skinned people changed places, silently, instantly, without the slightest preparation, without the slightest follow-through.

"—that we're a little faster on the draw than you are," Brand finished from his new position, evenly, but his voice smiting Carl's other ear like a final insult. "We need no other weapons. Dig me?"

"Yulp," Carl said. As a final word, it was not much better than his first.

The sheathed man led him out the oval door.

2

Numb as he had thought he was by now to everything but his own alarm, Carl was surprised to be surprised by the spaciousness of what they had called "the cages". His section of them reminded him more of an executive suite, or his imaginings of one—a large single bedroom, a wardrobe, a bathroom, and a sort of office containing a desk with a small TV screen and a headset like a cross between a hairdrier and set of noise-mufflers.

He had been marched to this in total silence by the silver man, through a long corridor where they had passed several others of the metal people, all of whom had passed them by wordlessly and with their eyes as blanked out as Little Orphan Annie's. Once they had arrived at the cage, however, Brand had turned affable, showing him the facilities, even including a stock of clean clothes, and seating him at last at the desk.

"I'll talk to you further when there's more time," the silver man said. "At the moment we're still recruiting. If you want food, you can call for it through that phone. I hope you know that you can't get away. If you cut out of the cage, there'd be no place where you could wind up."

Brand reached forward to the desk and touched something. Under Carl's feet, a circular area about the size of a snow-slider turned transparent, and Carl found himself looking down at the Bay area through nothing but ten miles or more of thin air. Even moderate heights had always made him sick; he clutched at the edge of the desk and was just about to lose his option when the floor turned solid again.

"I wanted you to see," Brand said, "that you really are aboard our ship. By the way, if you'd like to look through there again, the button for it's right here."

"Thanks," Carl said, calling up one of his suavest witticisms, "but no thanks."

"Suit yourself. Is there anything else you'd like, until we meet again?"

"Well . . . you said you were bringing more, uh, Earth people up here. If you could bring my wife . . .?"

The answer to this was of any academic interest to Carl. He had been separated from Bea for more than a year, ever since the explosion about college; and on the whole it had been painless, since they had been civilized enough to have been married in the first place only at common law and that a little bit by accident. But it would have been nice to have had someone he knew up here, if only somebody with a reasonably pink skin. The silver man said:

"Sorry. None of the other males we expect to bring aboard will know you, or each other. We find it better to follow the same rule with females, so we won't have any seizures of possessiveness."

He got up and moved towards the door, which was the usual shape for doors, not oval like the last one. He still seemed relatively gracious, but at the door he turned and added:

"We want you to understand from the outset that up here you own nobody—and nobody owns you but us." And with that, in a final silent non-explosion of arrogance, he flicked into nothingness, leaving Carl staring with glazed eyes at the unbroached door.

Of course no warning could have prevented Carl, or anyone else above the mental level of a nematode, from trying to think about escape; and Carl, because he had been selected as the one lay volunteer to visit the spaceship possibly because he had thought about spaceships now and then or read about them, thought he ought to be able to work out some sort of plan—if only he could stop jittering for a few minutes. In order to compose his mind, he got undressed and into the provided pyjamas—the first time he had worn such an outfit in ten years—and ordered the ship (through the desk phones) to send him a bottle of muscatel, which arrived promptly out of a well in the centre of the desk. To test the ship's good will, he ordered five other kinds of drink, and got them all, some of which he emptied with conscious self-mastery down the toilet.

Then he thought, jingling a luxurious bourbon-and-ginger abstractedly; the sound of ice was peculiarly comforting. Why the hell *had* the Pentagon people picked him as the "lay volunteer", out of so many? The alien ship had asked for a sampling of human beings to go back to its far star, and of these, it had wanted one to be a man of no specialties whatsoever—or no specialties that the ship had been willing to specify. The Pentagon had picked its own sampling of experts, who probably had been ordered to "volunteer"; but the "lay volunteer" had been another matter.

Like everyone else, Carl had been sure the Pentagon would want the "lay volunteer" actually to be a master spy among all possible master spies, not a James Bond but a Leamy type, a man who could pass for anything; but it hadn't worked that way. Instead, the Pentagon had approved Carl, one slightly beat and more than slightly broke dropout, who believed in magic and the possibility of spaceships, but—let us face it, monsters and gents—didn't seem to be of much interest either to alien or to human otherwise.

Why, for instance, hadn't the "lay volunteer" the aliens wanted turned out to be a Bircher, a Black Muslim, a Communist or a Rotarian—in short, some kind of fanatic who purported to deal with the *real* world—instead of a young man who was fanatic only about imaginary creatures called hobbits? Even an ordinary science-fiction fan would have been better; why was a sword-and-sorcery addict required to try to figure his way out of a classical spaceship clink?

Gradually, he began to feel—with pain, and only along the edges—that there was an answer to that. He got up and began to pace, which took him into the bedroom. Once there, he sat down nervously on the bed.

At once, the lights went out. Wondering if he had inadvertently sat on a trigger, he stood up again; but the darkness persisted.

Were the metal people reading his mind again—and trying to suppress any further thinking? It might well work. He was damn-all tired, and he'd been out of practice at thinking anyhow. Well, he could lie down and pretend to be asleep. Maybe that would—

The lights went on.

Though he was dead sure that he hadn't fallen asleep, he knew that he was rested. He remembered that when he had looked down the sink-hole under the desk, lights had been

coming on around the Bay. Gritting his teeth and swallowing
to keep down the anticipated nausea, he went out to the
desk and touched the button.

One glance was enough, luckily. It was high morning on
Earth. A night had passed.

And what was the thought he had lost? He couldn't remember. The ship had finessed him—as easily as turning a
switch.

3

He ordered breakfast; the ship delivered it. The bottles
and glasses, he noticed, had been taken away. As an insulting
aftermath, the ship also ran him another bath without his
having ordered it. He took it, since he saw nothing to be
gained by going dirty up here; it would be as unimpressive
as carrying a poster around that sink-hole. No razor was
provided; evidently the ship didn't object to his beard.

He then went after a cigarette, couldn't find any, and
finally settled for a slow burn, which was easy enough to
muster from all his deprivations, but somehow wasn't as
satisfying as usual. *I'll show them*, he thought; but show
them what? They looked invulnerable—and besides, he had
no idea what they wanted him for; all the official clues had
been snatched away, and no substitutes provided.

How about making a play for Lavelle? *That* would show
that chrome-plated s.o.b. But how to get to her? And again,
show him what? Carl knew nothing about these people's
sexual taboos; they might just not give a damn, like most
Earth people on shipboard. And besides, the girl seemed
pretty formidable. But lush; it would be fun to break her
down. He'd been through stuffier chicks in his time: Bea,
for instance, or—well, Bea, for instance. And the separation
hadn't really been his fault—

His stomach twinged and he got up to pace. The trouble
was that he had nothing to impress Lavelle with but his

build, which really wasn't any better than Brand's. His encyclopedic knowledge of the habits of hobbits wasn't going to crush any buttercups around here, and he doubted that being able to sing *Fallout Blues* in two separate keys would, either. Dammit, they'd left him nothing to *work* with! It was unfair.

Abruptly remembering last night's drinks, he stopped at the desk and tried asking for cigarettes. They materialized instantly. Well, at least the aliens weren't puritans—that was hopeful. Except that he didn't want a complaisant Lavelle; that wouldn't show anybody anything, least of all himself. There was no particular kick in swingers.

But if they gave him drinks and butts, they might just let him roam about, too. Maybe there was somebody else here that he could use, or some other prisoner who could give him clues. For some reason the thought of leaving the cage sparked a brief panic, but he smothered it by thinking of the ship as a sort of convention hotel, and tried the door.

It opened as readily as the entrance to a closet. He paused on the threshold and listened, but there was absolutely no sound except the half-expected hum of machinery. Now the question was, supposing the opening of the door had been an accident, and he was *not* supposed to be prowling around the ship? But that was their worry, not his; they had no right to expect him to obey their rules. Besides, as Buck Rogers used to say under similar circumstances, there was only one way to find out.

There was no choice of direction, since the corridor's ends were both unknown. Moving almost soundlessly—one real advantage of tennis shoes—he padded past a succession of cage doors exactly like his own, all closed and with no clues for guessing who or what lay behind them. Soon, however, he became aware that the corridor curved gently to the right; and just after the curve passed the blind point, he found himself on the rim of a park.

Startled, he shrank back, then crept forward still more

cautiously. The space down the ramp ahead was actually a long domed hall or auditorium, oval in shape, perhaps five city blocks in length and two across at the widest point, which was where the opening off the corridor debouched. It seemed to be about ten storeys high at the peak, floored with grass and shrubbery, and rimmed with small identical patios —one of which, he realized with a dream-like lack of surprise, must back up against his own cage. It all reminded him unpleasantly of one of those enlightened zoos in which animals are allowed to roam in spurious freedom in a moated "ecological setting".

As he looked down into the park, there was a long sourceless sigh like a whisper of metal leaves, and doors opened at the back of each patio. Slowly, people began to come out— pink people, not metal ones. He felt a brief mixture of resentment and chagrin; had he stayed in his own cage, he would have been admitted to the park automatically now, without having to undergo the jumpy and useless prowl down the companionway.

Anyway, he had found fellow prisoners, just as he had hoped; and it would be safer down there than up here. He loped eagerly downhill.

The ramp he was following ran between two patios. One of them was occupied by a girl, seated upon a perfectly ordinary camp chair and reading. He swerved, braking.

"Well, hi there!" he said.

She looked up, smiling politely but not at all as pleased to see another inmate as he could have hoped. She was small, neat and smoky, with high cheekbones and black hair— perhaps a Latin Indian, but without the shyness he usually counted upon with such types.

"Hello," she said. "What have they got you in for?"

That he understood; it was a standard jailhouse question.

"I'm supposed to be the resident science-fiction fan," he said, in an unusual access of humility. "Or that's my best guess. My name's Carl Wade. Are you an expert?"

"I'm Jeanette Hilbert. I'm a meteorologist. But as a reason for my being here, it's obviously a fake—this place has about as much weather as a Zeppelin hangar. Apparently it's the same story with all of us."

"How long have you been here?"

"Two weeks, I think. I wouldn't swear to it."

"So long? I was snatched only last night."

"Don't count on it," Jeanette said. "Time is funny here. These metal people seem to jump all around in it—or else they can mess with your memory at will."

Carl remembered the change in the clock face, back when Brand and Lavelle had been showing off their powers for him. It hadn't occurred to him that time rather than space might have been involved, despite that clue. He wished he had read more Hubbard—something about transfer of *theta* from one MEST entity to another—no, he couldn't recapture the concept, which he had never found very illuminating anyhow. Korzybski? Madame Blavatsky? The hell with it. He said:

"How'd you come on board?"

"Suddenly. I was taken right out of my apartment, a day after NASA volunteered me. Woke up in an EEG lab here, having my brain-prints taken."

"So did I. Hmm. Any fuzzy period between?"

"No, but that doesn't prove anything." She looked him over, slowly and deliberately. It was not an especially approving glance. "Is that what science-fiction fans usually wear?"

He was abruptly glad that his levis and shirt were at least clean, no matter how willy-nilly. "Work clothes," he explained.

"Oh. What kind of work?"

"Photography," he said, masking a split-second's groping with his most winning smile. It was, he knew a workable alias; most girls dream of posing. "But they didn't bring my cameras and stuff along with me, so I guess I'm as useless as you are, really."

"Oh," she said, getting up, "I'm not sure I'm so useless. I didn't bring my barometer, but I still have my head."

Dropping her book on the chair, she swung away and went back into her cage, moving inside her simple dress as flexibly as a reed.

"Hey, Jeanette—I didn't mean—just a——"

Her voice came back: "They close the doors again after an hour." Then, as if in mockery, her own door closed behind her, independently.

For want of anything else to do, he stepped into the patio and picked up the book. It was called *Experimental Design*, by one Sir Ronald Fisher, and the first sentence that he hit read: "In fact, the statement can be made that the probability that the unknown mean of the population is less than a particular limit, is exactly P, namely $Pr\,(u < \bar{x} + ts) = P$ for all values of P, where t is known (and has been tabulated as a function of P and N)." He dropped the thin volume hastily. He had been wondering vaguely whether Jeanette had brought the book with her or the ship had supplied it, but suddenly he couldn't care less. It began to look as though all the chicks he encountered on this ship had been born to put him down.

Disappointed at his own indifference, he remembered her warning, and looked quickly back at the top of the gangway down which he had come. It was already closed. Suppose he was cut off? There were people down there in the park that he still wanted to talk to—but obviously not now. He raced along the esplanade.

He identified his own cage almost entirely by intuition; and it seemed that he was scarcely in it five minutes before the door to the patio slid shut. Now he had something else to think about, and he was afraid to try it, not only because it was painful, but because despite Jeanette's theories about time and memory, he still thought it very likely that Lavelle and her consort could read his mind. Experience, after all, supported all three theories indifferently, thus far.

But what about the *other* door? Increasingly it seemed to him that he hadn't been intended to go through it. He had been told that he couldn't get out of his cage; and the one hour's access to the park was nothing more than admission to a larger cage, not any sort of permission to roam. The unlocked outer door had to have been an accident. And if so, and if it were still open, there should still be all sorts of uses he might make of it—

He froze, waiting to be jumped into the next day by the mind-readers. Nothing happened. Perhaps they could read his mind, but weren't doing it at the moment. They couldn't be reading everybody's mind every minute of the day; they were alien and powerful, but also very obviously human in many important ways. All right. Try the outer door again. There was really nothing in the world that he wanted to do less, but the situation was beginning to make him mad, and rage was the only substitute he had for courage.

And after all, what could they do to him if they caught him, besides knock him out? The hell with them. Here goes.

Once more, the door opened readily.

4

The corridor was as eventless as ever; the ramp to the park now closed. He continued along the long smooth curve, which obviously skirted the park closely, just outside the cage doors. Once he stopped to lay his ear to one of the cages. He heard nothing, but he did notice a circle with a pattern of three holes in it, like a diagram of a bowling ball, just where the lock to an ordinary door would be placed for someone of Brand's height.

That made him think again as he prowled. So the metal people needed handles and locks! Then they couldn't jump about in space as magically as they wanted you to think they could. Whatever the trick was, it wasn't teleportation or time-travel. It was an illusion, or something else to do with the mind, as both Carl and Jeanette had guessed: memory-blanking, or mind-reading. But which?

After he had crept along for what seemed like a mile, the elliptical pathway inflected and began to broaden. Also, there was a difference in the quality of the light up ahead: it seemed brighter, and, somehow, more natural. The ceiling was becoming higher, too. He was coming into a new kind of area; and for some reason he did not stop to examine—perhaps only that the inside curve of the corridor was on his right, which as evidence was good for nothing—he felt that he was coming up on the front of the ship.

He had barely begun to register the changes when the corridor put forth a pseudopod: a narrow, shallow metal stairway which led up to what looked like the beginning of a catwalk, off to the left. He detoured instinctively—in the face of the unknown, hide and peek!

As he went along the outward-curving catwalk, the space ahead of him continued to grow bigger and more complicated, and after a few minutes he saw that his sensation that he was going bowwards had been right. The catwalk ran up and around a large chamber, shaped like a fan opened from this end, and ending in an immense picture window through which daylight poured over a cascade of instruments. On the right side of the room was a separate, smaller bank of controls, divided into three ranks of buttons each arranged in an oval, and surmounted by a large clock-face like the one Carl had noticed when he first awoke in the ship's EEG room. The resemblance to the cockpit of a jetliner, writ large, was unmistakable; this was the ship's control room.

But there was something much more important to see. Brand—or someone almost exactly like him—was sitting in one of two heavy swivel seats in front of the main instrument board, his silver skin scattering the light from the window into little wavelets all over the walls to either side of him. Occasionally he leaned forward and touched something, but in the main he did not seem to have much to do at the moment. Carl had the impression that he was waiting, which the little flicks of motion only intensified—like a cat watching a rubber mouse.

Carl wondered how long he had been there. From the quality of the light, the time was now either late morning or early afternoon—it was impossible to guess which, since Carl could not read the alien clock.

A movement to the right attracted both men's attention. It was a black-metalled woman: Lavelle. Of this identification Carl was dead sure, for he had paid much closer attention to her than to her consort. Lifting a hand in greeting, she came forward and sat down in the other chair, and the two began to talk quietly, their conversation interspersed with occasional bursts of low laughter which made Carl uncomfortable for some reason he did not try to analyse. Though he could catch frequent strings of syllables and an occasional whole sentence, the language was not English, Spanish or French, the only ones he was equipped to recognize; but it was quite liquid, unlike a Germanic or Slavic tongue. Ship's language, he was certain.

Their shadows grew slowly longer on the deck; then it must be afternoon. That double prowl up the corridor must have taken longer than he had thought. He was just beginning to feel hungry when there was a change that made him forget his stomach completely.

As the metal people talked, their voices had been growing quieter and a little more husky. Now, Brand leaned forward and touched the board again, and instantly, like flowers unfolding in stop-motion photography, the metal suits— aha, they *were* suits!—unpeeled around them and seemed to dissolve into the chairs, leaving them both entirely nude.

Now would be the time to jump them, except that he was quite certain he couldn't handle both of them. Instead, he simply watched, grateful for the box seat. There was something about the girl besides her nudity that was disquieting, and after a while Carl realized what it was. Except for her baldness, she bore a strong resemblance to the first girl he had ever made time with by pretending to be a photographer, a similarity emphasized by the way she was sitting in the chair.

Obviously the pose was not lost on Brand, either. He got to his feet with a lithe motion, and seizing her hand, pulled her to her feet. She went to him freely enough, but after a moment struggled away, laughing, and pointed at the smaller control board, the one with the clock. Brand made an explosive remark, and then, grinning, strode over to the board and

the room was dark and empty. Blinking amazedly, Carl tried to stir, and found that his muscles were completely cramped, as if he had been lying on the metal ledge in the same position all night.

Just like that, he had the key in his hands.

He began to work out the stiffness slowly, starting with fingers and toes, and surveying the control room while he did so. The room was not really completely dark ; there were many little stars gleaming on the control boards, and a very pale dawn was showing through the big window. The large hand on the clock face had jumped a full ninety degrees widdershins.

When he felt ready to take on a fight if he had to—except for his hunger, about which he could do nothing—Carl went back to the stairs and down into the control room, going directly to the smaller of the two boards. There was no doubt in his mind now about what those three ovals of buttons meant. If there was any form of dialogue he understood no matter what the language, it was the dialogue of making out. As plain as plain, the last two lines the denuded metal people had spoken had gone like this :

LAVELLE : But suppose somebody (my husband, the captain, the doctor, the boss) should come in?

BRAND: Oh hell, I'll (lock the door, take the phone off the hook, put out the lights) fix that!

Blackout.

What Brand had done was to put everyone on board to sleep. Out of the suits, he and Lavelle must have been immune to whatever effect he had let loose, so that they could play their games at leisure. A neat trick; Carl wouldn't mind learning it—and he thought he was about to.

Because Carl himself was awake now, it was pretty clear that the other prisoners were also; maybe they had been freed automatically by the passage of the clock past a certain point in the morning, and would be put back to sleep just as automatically after supper. It also seemed clear that for the prisoners, the effect didn't depend upon wearing one of the metal suits or being in the cages, since Carl had been knocked out up on the catwalk, almost surely unsuspected. The suits must be the captain's way of controlling the crew —and that meant that Brand (or Brand and Lavelle) must run the shop, since this board was too powerful to allow just anybody to fool with it. Carl rubbed his hands together.

One of these three circles must represent the crew; another, the cages; the third—well, there was no telling who was controlled by those buttons—maybe crew and prisoners at once. But the oval in the middle had the fewest number of buttons, so it was probably a safe bet that it controlled the cages. But how to test that?

Taking a deep breath, Carl systematically pressed each and every button on the left-hand oval. Nothing happened. Since he himself was not now sprawled upon the deck, unconscious again, he could now assume that the crew was once more fast asleep—with the unavoidable exception of any who had been out of their suits, like the lovers.

Now for the sparser oval. Trying to remind himself that he now had plenty of time, Carl worked out by painful memory and counting upon his fingers just where the button which represented his cage probably was. Then, starting one button away from it, he again went all around the circle until he was one button on the opposite side of what he thought was his own.

It took him a long time, sweating, to work himself up to touching either of those two bracketing buttons, but at last, holding his breath, he pressed them both at once, watching the clock as he did so.

He did not fall and the clock did not jump.

The ship was his.

He was not in the slightest doubt about what he was going to do with it. He had old scores by the millions to pay off, and was going to have himself one hell of a time doing it, too. With an instrument like this, no power on Earth could stop him.

Of course he'd need help: somebody to figure out the main control board with him, somebody with a scientific mind and some technical know-how, like Jeanette. But he'd pick his help damn carefully.

The thought of Jeanette made him feel ugly, a sensation he rather enjoyed. She'd been damn snippy. There might be other women in the cages, too; and the aborted scene of last night in the control room had left him feeling more frustrated than usual. All right; first some new scores, and then he'd get around to the old ones.

5

It was high morning when he got back to the control room, but still it was earlier than he'd expected it to be. There hadn't been many women in the cages, but either they got less and less attractive as he went along, or the recent excitement and stress had taken more out of him physically than he'd realized. Otherwise he was sure he could have completed such a programme handily, maybe even twice around. Oh well, there was plenty of time. Now he needed help.

The first thing to do was to disconnect the clock in some way. That proved to be easy: a red bar under it simply stopped it. Since nobody, obviously, had visited the control room since his last tampering, he now had the whole ship in permanent coma.

Next, he counted down to Jeanette's button and pushed it. That ought to awaken her. The only remaining problem was to work out how that three-hole lock on her cage worked.

That didn't turn out to be easy at all. It took an hour of fumbling before it suddenly sank inward under his hand and the door slid back.

Jeanette was dressed, and stared at him with astonishment. "How did you do that?" she said. "What's wrong with the phone? Where's the food? Have you been doing something stupid?"

He was just about to lash back at her when he realized that this was no time to start the breaking-off routine, and instead put on his best master-of-the-situation smile, as if he were just starting up with her.

"Not exactly," he said. "But I've got control of the ship. Mind if I come in?"

"Control of the ship? But—well, all right, come in. You're in anyhow."

He came forward and sat down at her version of his desk. She backed away from him, only a little, but quite definitely. "Explain yourself," she said.

He didn't; but he told her the rudiments of the story, in as earnest and forthright manner as he had ever managed to muster in his life. As he had expected, she asked sharp technical questions, most of which he parried, and her superior manner dissolved gradually into one of intense interest.

All the same, whenever he made the slightest movement to stand up, she stepped slightly away from him, a puzzled expression flitting across her face and then vanishing again as he fed her new details. He was puzzled in turn. Though the enforced ship's-sleep hadn't prevented her from being highly responsive—in fact, it was his guess that it had helped —he was sure that she had never awakened even for a second during the morning and hence had nothing to blame him for. Yet it was obvious that she knew, somewhere in the back of her mind, that *something* happened to her, and associated it with him. Well, maybe that would be helpful too, in the long run; a cut cake goes stale in a hurry.

When he was through, she said reluctantly: "That was close observation, and quick thinking."

"Not very quick. It took me all morning to work it out."

Again the flitting, puzzled expression. "You got the right answer in time. That's as quick as anybody needs to be. Did you wake anybody else?"

"No, just you. I don't know anybody else here, and I figured you could help me. Besides, I didn't want a mob of released prisoners running around the ship kicking the crew and fooling with things."

"Hmm. Also sensible. I must say, you surprise me." Carl couldn't resist a grin at this, but took care to make it look bashful. "Well—what do you suggest we do now?"

"We ought to figure out the main control board. See if it's possible for us to run the ship without anybody from the crew to help—and how many hands from the cages we'd need to do the job."

"Yes," she said thoughtfully. "At a guess, the main control board is as rational as the sleep-board is. And the two captains—Brand and Lavelle—must be able to run the ship from there all by themselves in a pinch; otherwise the threat of knocking all the rest of the crew out wouldn't have sufficient force. Interesting social system these people must have. I don't think I like them."

"Me neither," Carl said with enthusiasm. "I hate people who whip serfs."

Jeanette's eyebrows rose. "The crew can't be serfs. They

wear the metal suits—a powerful tool in any hands—and can take them off whenever they like if they want to duck the sleep-compulsion. But obviously they don't. They can't be serfs; they must be something like chattel slaves, who'd never dream of changing status except to other owners. But that's not nearly the most interesting problem."

"What is, then?"

"How the buttons put *us* to sleep. We don't wear the suits."

Since this was the problem Carl most badly wanted to solve secretly and for himself alone, it was the one he most badly wanted Jeanette not to think about; yet since he had no clues at all, he had to chance at least a tentative sounding before trying to divert her from it. He said: "Any ideas?"

"Not at the moment. Hmm. . . . Did you have a headache when you first woke up on board?"

"I've got it still," he said, patting the back of his neck tenderly. "Why? Does that signify?"

"Probably not. I'll just have to look at the board, that's all. We'd better go take a thorough look around."

"Sure. This way."

She was very thorough—exasperatingly so. Long after he would have been sure that he had seen everything, she would return to some small instrument complex she had looked at three or four times before, and go over it again as if she had never seen it before. She volunteered nothing except an occasional small puff of surprise or interest; and to his questions, she replied uniformly, "I don't know yet." Except once, when after she had bent over a panel of travelling tapes for what must have been twenty minutes, she had said instead, "Shut up for ten seconds, will you?"

In the meantime, the sun was reddening towards afternoon again, and Carl was becoming painfully conscious of the fact that he had had nothing to eat since breakfast the day before. Every minute added without any food shortened his temper, reduced his attention span and cut into his patience. Maybe the girl was getting results, and maybe not, but he was more and more sure that she was putting him on. Didn't she know who was boss here?

Maybe she thought she could make a dash for the sleep-panel and turn *him* off. If she tried that, he would knock her down. He had never been that far away from the panel; he was on guard.

Suddenly she straightened from the main board and sat down in one of the heavy swivel chairs. It promptly began to peel her clothes off. Though he had not told her anything about this trick, she got up so quickly that it left her only slightly shredded around the edges. She eyed the chair thoughtfully, but said nothing. For some reason this was her most galling silence of all.

"Got anything?" he said harshly.

"Yes, I think so. These controls require an optimum of three people, but two can run them in an emergency. Ordinarily I think they use five, but two of those must be standbys."

"Could one man handle them?"

"Not a chance. There are really three posts here: pilot, engineer, navigator. The pilot and the navigator can be the same person if it's absolutely necessary. Nobody can substitute for the engineer. This ship runs off a Nernst-effect generator, a very tricky form of hydrogen fusion. The generators idle very nicely, but when they're drawing real power they have to be watched—more than that, it takes a real musician's hand to play them."

"Could you do it?"

"I'd hate to have to try. Maybe with a month of ant-steps, saying 'May I' all the way. But if the thing blew at this altitude it'd take out the whole West coast—at a minimum. There's an awful lot of hydrogen in the Pacific; I wouldn't answer for what a Nernst fireball would really start."

"Good."

She swung on him, her brows drawing together. "What's good about it? What are you up to, anyhow?"

"Nothing very awful," he said, trying to be placating. "I'll tell you in a minute. First of all, have you figured out how to get the grub moving again? I'm starving."

"Yes, that's what the third oval on the sleep-board is—the phone system locks. There's a potentiometer system on the side of the board that chooses what's activated—food, phones, doors, and so on. If you'll move over a minute, I'll show you."

"In a minute," he said. "It's not that I don't trust you, Jeanette, but you know how it is—now that I've got my mitts on this thing, I hate to let go of it."

"That figures. What are you going to do with it?"

"I don't know till I've got it doped better. First, how about this business of putting the prisoners crumped without any suits?"

"No," she said.

"Whadd'ya mean, no?" he said, feeling the ugliness rise again. "Listen, chick——"

He caught himself, but with an awful feeling that it was too late. She watched him damping himself down with sober amusement, and then said:

"Go on. That was the true hyena laugh."

He clenched his fists, and again fought himself back to normal, aware that she was observing every step of the process. He said:

"I'm sorry. I'm tired and hungry. I'll try not to snarl at you again. Okay?"

"Okay." But she said nothing more.

"So what about this crump effect?"

"Sorry. I won't answer any more questions until you've answered one of mine. It's very simple. Once you've really got control of the ship—and you can't get it without me— what do you plan to do with it? You keep telling me you'll tell me 'in a minute'. Tell me now."

"All right," he said, his teeth on edge. "All right. Just remember that you asked me for it. If you don't like it, tough tibby—it's not my fault. I'm going to use this ship and everybody in it to set things straight. The warmongers, the bluenoses, the fuzz, the snobs, the squares, the bureaucrats, the Uncle Toms, the Birchers, the Fascists, the rich-bitches, the . . . everybody who's ever been *against* anything is going to get it now, right in the neck. I'm going to tear down all the vested interests, from here to Tokyo. If they go along with me, okay. If they don't, blooey! If I can't put 'em to sleep I can blow 'em up. I'm going to strike out for freedom for *everybody*, in all directions, and all at once. There'll never be a better chance. There'll never be a better weapon than this ship. And there'll never be a better man than me to do it."

His voice sank slightly. The dream was catching hold. "You know damn well what'd happen if I let this ship get taken over by the Pentagon or the fuzz. They'd suppress it—hide it—make a weapon out of it. It'd make the cold war worse. And the sleep gadget—they'd run all our lives with it. Sneak up on us. Jump in and out of our pads. Spy. All the rest. Right now's our chance to do justice with it. And that by God is what I'm going to do with it!"

"Why you?" Jeanette said. Her voice sounded very remote.

"Because I know what the underdog goes through. I've gone through it all. I've been put down by every kind of slob that walks the Earth. And I've got a long memory. I remember every one of them. Every one. In my mind, every one of them has a front name, a hind name, and an address. With a thing like this ship, I can track every man jack of them down and pay them off. No exceptions. No hiding. No mercy. Just justice. The real, pure, simple thing."

"Sounds good."

"You bet it's good!"

"What about the Soviets? I missed them on your list, somehow."

"Oh sure ; I hate Communists. And also the militarists—it

177

was the Pentagon that sucked us into this mess up here to begin with, you know that. Freedom for everybody—at one stroke!"

She seemed to consider that. "Women, too?"

"Of course, women! The hell with the double standard! On both sides!"

"I don't quite follow you," she said. "I thought the double standard only had one side—the men could and the women couldn't."

"You know damn well that's not so. It's the women who control the situation—they always can, they're the ones who get to say *no*. The real freedom is all on their side."

"How'd you fix that?" she said, in a voice almost sleepy.

"I . . . well, I haven't had much of a chance to think about it——"

"I think you've thought about it quite a lot."

Her shredded dress trailing streamers, Jeanette walked steadily away from the control board towards the corridor. Carl put his finger over her button.

"Stop!"

She stopped and turned, shielding her thighs with one hand in a peculiarly modest gesture, considering everything. "Well?"

"I don't give a damn what you think. If you don't dig it, that's your nuisance—sorry about that, Chief. But I need you; I'll have you."

"No you won't. You can put me to sleep and rape me, but you won't have me."

"Yes I will. I can wake you up. And I won't feed you. You'll spend all the rest of your time in your cage—hungry and wide awake. In the meantime, *I'll* fool with the boards. Maybe I'll wake somebody else who'll be willing to help. Maybe even one of the crew. Or maybe I'll make a mistake and blow everything up—if you weren't putting me on about that. Think about *that* for a while. Co-operate, or blooey! How about that?"

"I'll think about it," she said. But she went right on walking.

Carl bit his tongue savagely and turned back to the main boards. These goddam do-gooders. In the pinch, they were all alike. Give them a chance to *do* something, and they chickened out.

Now it was up to him. It would be nice to know where to find Lavelle. But it was nicer to be sure that Jeanette had him dead wrong. He had a mission now and was above that stuff, at least for the time being. Once he'd reduced the world, he could do better than either of them. Mmmmm.

Raging with hunger, he scraped his fingernails at the powerful little lights.

6

But he had at last to admit that much of his threat had been simple bravado. The instruments and controls on the board were in obviously related groups, but without technical training he could not even figure out the general categories; and though everything was labelled, the very script the labels were written in was as unbreakable to him as an oscilloscope trace (which it strongly resembled).

Besides, his thinking was obviously not being improved by his having been without a meal for more than a whole day. He decided that he had better be reasonable. The only other course was to wake some crew member, on the chance that a random choice would net him a slave rather than an officer, and try to force him to read the inscriptions; but the risks in that were obvious and frightening. Unless he really wanted to blow up the joint—which in fact he had no intention of chancing—he had to make another try with Jeanette.

She didn't look nearly as haggard as he had hoped, but after all she had both eaten and slept a good deal more recently than he had. Realizing at the same time that he was not only haggard, but untrimmed and dirty, he made an extra effort to be plausible.

"Look, I'm sorry I frightened you. I'm tired, I'm hungry, and I'm on edge. Let's try to talk it all over again sensibly, like civilized people."

"I don't talk to jailers," she said coldly.

"I don't blame you. On the other hand, as long as you're bucking me, I have to keep some sort of control over you. You're the only other prisoner who knows as much as I know. Hell, you know *more* than I know about some things."

"The last I heard, you weren't just going to keep me locked up. You were going to torture me."

"What? I said no such——"

"No sleep, no food—what do you call it? Punishment? Persuasion? I know what I call it."

"All right," he said. "I was wrong about that. Why don't we start there? You tell me how to turn the food deliveries back on, and I'll do it. There's no harm in that. We'd both benefit."

"That's right, you're hungry too. Well, it's controlled by that knob on the side of the sleep-board, as I told you. I'm not sure, but I think it's the third setting to the left—counter-clockwise, that is."

"Good. I'll see to it that you get fed, and then maybe we can yak again."

"Maybe."

At the door, he turned back suddenly. "This had better not be a gag. If that third setting wakes everybody up or something like that——"

"I don't guarantee a thing," Jeanette said calmly. "It's only my best guess. But I don't want the slavers awake again any more than you do. You're no picnic, but I like them even less."

The point was all the more penetrating for its bluntness. Back in the control room, he set the dial as per instructions, and then raced back to his own cage to try it out. The ship promptly delivered the meal he ordered, and he stuffed himself gorgeously. As an afterthought, he ordered and got a bottle of brandy. He was still determined to puzzle out the control boards as far as possible by himself, and in his present stage of exhaustion a little lubricant might make all the difference.

He knocked on Jeanette's door in passing, but there was no answer.

"Jeanette!" he shouted. "Jeanette, the food's on!"

Still no response. He wondered if the metal door would pass sound. Then, very faintly, he heard something like a whimper. After a long pause, there was another.

He went on, satisfied. He was a little surprised to find that she was able to cry—up to now she had seemed as hard as nails except in her sleep—but it would probably do her good. Besides, it was satisfying to know that she had a breaking point; it would make his persuasions all the more effective, in the long run. And in the meantime, she had heard him announce that there was food available, so she should have a little better opinion of his good faith.

He went on up the corridor, cheerfully whistling *Fallout Blues* in two keys at once.

The control room window showed deep night, and had for a long time, when he decided to call himself defeated—temporarily, of course. The brandy had calmed some of his jumpiness and done wonders for his self-confidence, but it hadn't brought into his head any technical knowledge or any safe inspirations, either. And suddenly he was reelingly sleepy. The headache was worse, too.

There should be no danger in catching a little sack time. Everybody else was already out except Jeanette, and she was locked in. Of course, she was a sharp apple, and might figure some way of getting out. It would be better to crump her. She'd probably appreciate it, too. It would give him two plusses to start the next conversation with.

181

He pressed the button that controlled her, and then, avoiding the strip-tease chairs, rolled himself comfortably under the big board.

He awoke slowly and naturally; he had almost forgotten how it felt, after the popped-out-of-nothingness effect that the ship's imposed awakenings produced, and for a little while he simply luxuriated in it. After all, there was no danger. The ship was his.

But it was unusually noisy this morning: a distant snarling of engines, an occasional even more distant murmur of voices—

Voices! He shot upright in alarm.

He was no longer aboard the ship.

Around him was the sunlit interior of a small room, unmistakably barracks-like, with a barred window, furnished only by the narrow single bed in which he had been lying. He himself was clad in grey military-hospital pyjamas, and touching his face, he found that he was clean-shaven—his beard was gone—and had been given a GI haircut. A standard maroon military-hospital robe was folded neatly over the foot of the bed.

An aircraft engine thrummed again outside. Swearing, he ran to the window.

He was indeed locked up beside a military airfield—which one, he had no way of telling, but at least it was American. It was also huge. There was a lot of traffic.

And there was the alien spaceship, right in front of him, grounded. It was probably as much as three miles away, but it was still so enormous as to cut off most of the horizon.

It had been captured—and Carl Wade with it.

He wasted no time wondering how it had been done, or lamenting the collapse of his fantasies, in which, he realized, he had never really believed. The only essential thing now was—*get away*!

182

He spun to the door, and finding it locked, rattled it furiously.

"Hey!" he shouted furiously. "Let me out of here! You've got no right—I'm a civilian—a citizen——"

The lock clicked under his hand, and as he jumped back, there was the hard sound of a bolt being shot. The door opened and Jeanette came in, followed by two large, impassive, alert Air Force policemen. The girl looked fresh and beautiful; but she too had had a close haircut, all on one side; and there was a massive surgical compress taped under that ear.

"Good morning," she said.

He continued to back away until he found himself sitting on the bed.

"I might of guessed," he said. "So you got the upper hand and sold out."

"Sold out?" she said, her eyes flashing. "I had nothing to sell. I couldn't use the ship properly. I turned it over to people who could. My own people—who else?"

"All right, then you chickened out," Carl said. "It's the same thing. What are you going to do with me?"

"They tell me you'll be questioned and let go. In your circles, nobody'd be likely to believe anything you say. Just in case any reporter looks you up, the Pentagon's arranged an interview with *Time*. They'll treat your remarks as science-fiction and that'll be the end of you as any sort of witness."

"And that's all?" he said, amazed.

"That's enough. You're not accused of any crime. Of course, I suspect you committed one against me—but considering that it didn't even wake me up, it can't have been much more than a token; just kid stuff."

This blow to his pride was almost more than he could take, but he was not going to try to set her straight with those two huge flics standing there. He said dully:

"How did you do it?"

183

"I figured out how the metal people induced sleep in us without our having to wear the metal suits. When they first took us on board, they installed a little broadcaster of the sleep-waves, surgically, right next to our skulls—under the right mastoid process. That was what that headache was."

Carl caressed his neck automatically. The headache was gone; all that was left was a neat and painless scar.

"But what did you do?"

"I took it out, with your help. When you turned the food service back on, I ordered a tough steak, and I got a sharp knife along with it. Awake, the metal people probably wouldn't have allowed that, but computers are brainless. So I cut the gadget out. As soon as I got the bleeding stopped, I went forward, found you asleep under the control board, and pressed *your* button. The rest was very simple."

He remembered the faint whimpers he had heard when he had passed her door that night. And he had thought she was softening up!

The worst of it was, in like circumstances he could never have done it. He was afraid of blood, especially his own.

"Jeanette. . . . *Why* did you do it?"

She was silent a long time. At last she said:

"Do you believe in God?"

"Of course not!" he said indignantly. "Do you?"

"I don't know whether I do or not. But there's one thing I was sure of, right from the start: You'd be a damn poor substitute."

Acknowledgements

A much shorter version of "A Style in Treason" was published in *Impulse*, March 1966, as "A Hero's Life"; that version © 1966 by *Impulse*. That same text plus a new prologue (not included in this book) and with the present title was published in *Galaxy*, June 1970; that version © 1970 by Universal Publishing and Distributing Corporation.

"The Writing of the Rat", first published in *Galaxy*, June 1956; © 1956 by Galaxy Publishing Corp.

"And Some Were Savages", first published in *Amazing Stories*, November 1960; © 1960 by Ziff-Davis Publishing Company.

"None so Blind", first published by *Fantasy & Science Fiction*, May 1962, as "Who's In Charge Here?"; © 1962 by Mercury Press, Inc.

"No Jokes on Mars", first published by *Fantasy & Science Fiction*, October 1965; © 1965 by Mercury Press, Inc.

"A Dusk of Idols", first published in *Amazing Stories*, March 1961; © 1961 by Ziff-Davis Publishing Company.

"How Beautiful with Banners", first published in *Orbit 1*; © 1966 by Berkley Publishing Corporation.

"Skysign", first published in *Analog*, May 1968; © 1968 by The Condé Nast Publications Inc.

THE QUINCUNX OF TIME

James Blish

THE DIRAC TRANSMITTER: the key to space – and time

The new communications device had one huge advantage over ultrawave or the faster-than-light ships that still take months to carry a message from Earth to the outlying worlds. Its transmissions could be picked up instantly, anywhere in the Universe.

With an expanding interstellar empire to administer, Captain Robin Weinbaum reckoned his job would become a whole lot easier.

Until the impossible happened. Someone started monitoring the Dirac transmissions – before they were made.

45p

THE TESTAMENT OF ANDROS

The best science fiction stories of James Blish

A disaster-investigator of the future – whose craft is the reading of dead men's minds . . .

A polluted dying Earth where power is in the hands of the almighty International Brotherhood of Sanitary Engineers . . .

Minute aquatic human colonists, genetically bred to settle an underwater world . . .

A woman space pioneer who unwittingly brings heterosexuality to the primeval life on Titan . . .

All this and more: the best of the best from one of the true giants of SF

60p

FALLEN STAR

James Blish

Invited to join an expedition to the North Pole, science writer Julian Cole expected nothing more exciting than the occasional polar bear.

But that was before he met his companions: the eccentric egomaniac Farmsworth and his outrageous wife, who could look sexy even in a parka and red flannel longjohns; Dr Wentz, trying to drown a mysterious past in suicidal alcoholism; and the crazy albino Elvers, whose own secret spanned 15000 years and half the solar system . . .

A secret more chilling than any arctic blizzard!

60p

HOW TO ORDER